Tlooth

Tlooth

HARRY MATHEWS

CARCANET

First published in Great Britain 1988 by
Carcanet Press Limited
208–212 Corn Exchange Buildings
Manchester M4 3BQ

Published in the USA 1987 by
Carcanet
198 Sixth Avenue
New York, NY 10013

British Library Cataloguing in Publication Data

Mathews, Harry
  Tlooth.
  I. Title
  813'.54[F]   PS3563.A8359

  ISBN 0-85635-765-0

The publisher acknowledges the financial
assistance of the Arts Council of Great Britain

Printed in England by SRP Ltd, Exeter

Tlooth

It is a mistake to regard one disease as more divine than another, since all is human and all divine.

HIPPOCRATES

Part One

A Disappointing Inning

Mannish Madame Nevtaya slowly cried "Fur bowls!" and the Fideist batter, alert to the sense behind the sound of her words, jogged toward first base. The wind from the northern steppe blew coldly on the close of our season.

The Fideist division received the camp's worst villains, and its team assembled their dregs. Among us Defective Baptists a love of baseball signified gentleness; among Fideists, cruelty. Consider their bloodthirsty team—

Left field: undertaker's assistant and caterer to necrophiles, Sydney Valsalva kidnaped infants for beheading.

Center field: Lynn Petomi, dentist, mutilated the mouths of patients.

Pitcher: Hilary Cheyne-Stokes, gynecologist, committed analagous crimes.

1st base: Tommy Withering, osteopath, flayed a younger brother.

Shortstop: Evelyn Roak, surgeon, supplied human fragments to a delicatessen and was arrested for scandalous amputations.*

(2nd base: Cecil Meli, nurse, had been jailed by mistake.)

---

*For example, removing, together with a troublesome spur of bone, the index and ring fingers of my left hand. I was then a violinist.

Right field: Lee Donders, grocer, transformed Roak's material into "Donders' Delicacies."

Catcher: Marion Gullstrand, obstetrician, tortured un-wed mothers.

3rd base: Leslie Auenbrugger, psychiatrist—the "Rest-room Bomber."

Valsalva had walked. Since I was catcher, I went out to the mound to say a few words of encouragement. The second batter grounded to shortstop, forcing Valsalva; the third struck out; and the Fideists' turn at bat would have ended with Withering's high foul if, failing to allow for the wind, I had not misjudged it. Withering singled on the next pitch.

I was thus obliged to execute my plan in the first inning of the game. Having foreseen the possibility, I drew a pre-pared ball from my chest protector to substitute it for the one in play.

I had made the ball myself. It was built around two unusual parts—a tiny battery and a pellet of dynamite. From each of the battery's outlets, a wire extended through the hair stuffing of the ball about halfway to the leather wrapper. The free ends of the wires, one of which passed through a firing cap fixed to the dynamite, were six millimeters apart, enough to prevent their junction at a mild impact but not at a sufficiently hard one. The dif-ference, which I had determined exactly, was that between a fast pitch caught and a slow pitch hit. The wire ends separated into meshing sprays of filament, so that no matter how the ball was struck, it was certain to explode.

To shield myself, I had reinforced my equipment with layers of nylon in the chest protector, steel in the cap and shin guards, and a lucite screen inside the mask.

For the umpire's protection I counted on her thick skin. I expected the explosion to create general confusion, stun and knock down the batter, and explain the batter's death. The bomb itself would kill no one, but I had concealed in my right shin guard, ready to use as soon as the ball had been detonated, a hypodermic of botulin.

Evelyn Roak stood at the plate. To my dismay, the first three pitches were low—our pitcher later complained that the ball was heavy. The fourth was a perfect strike, and my hopes revived. At the next delivery the batter drew back to swing, but the pitch was wild. The ball sailed past my outstretched glove as I lunged at it, skittered over the ground behind home plate, off the playing field altogether, at last disappearing irretrievably, and with an abysmal liquid reverberation, into a drain.

My Dental Apprenticeship

The camp, in which I was completing my second year, had kept its prerevolutionary structure through historical, ideological and geographic change. Established during the Holy Alliance for the internment of heretics, it had since the eighties received offenders of every sort. Recently it had been transplanted intact, down to the last dossier, prisoner and guard, to its present southerly location at Jacksongrad.

The organization of the camp was sectarian. On arrival, prisoners were arbitrarily and finally committed to the Americanist, Darbyist, Defective Baptist, Fideist or Resurrectionist division. Although the assignments were theologically haphazard, the divisions had real unity. Particular types flourished in the various sects and were perhaps knowingly allotted to them; and the descendants of the first religious prisoners, faithful to their traditions, exerted a constant influence on their fellows.

This influence was strengthened by a ban on all political and nonconformist discussion, and by a strict segregation of the sects. Fideists and Resurrectionists, Americanists and Darbyists met only on exceptional occasions, such as

concerts, civic debates and athletic encounters. Even then
the guards held intercourse to a minimum, and the mere
exchange of greetings was beset with obstacles and penal-
ties.

Such circumstances had determined the plan so unsuc-
cessfully executed at the Fideist ball game. The stratagem
was not my first.

When, soon after my arrival, the camp authorities had
asked me to choose a professional activity, I had refused.
Because I was a musician I was urged to join the camp
orchestra, band or choir; but I had been too recently
maimed to take up the euphonium or sing hymns. The
cultural administrator, irked by my refusal, had relegated
me to the dental infirmary.

This was meant as a punishment but proved a boon.
The clinic had an evil reputation in the camp; but this
reflected, more than its drabness and inadequate equipment,
the mentality of its director, a martinet who spared neither
his patients nor his assistants. When I reported for work,
this person had just been replaced by a kind and intelligent
woman dentist, Dr. Zarater. She had been appointed by
the authorities to apply a more humane policy, and she
was empowered to reorganize the clinic accordingly.

My relations with Dr. Zarater were good from the start.
She at once remarked on the fitness of my left hand, reduced to three spaced digits, for working inside the mouth.
"No tool," she said, "is as good as a finger, but with five
it's like using your foot." She questioned me tactfully
about my mishap, then about my life. When I mentioned
in the course of our talk the name of R. King Dri, Dr.
Zarater's interest quickened; for she herself had studied
with Dr. King Dri and planned to use her clinic to demonstrate his methods.

Who was R. King Dri? I had learned of him by chance

some years before when, in a dentist's waiting room, I came across a letter about him in an old issue of *Dental Cosmos*.

King Dri called himself the "Philosopher-Dentist." Victim of a history of dental disorders that classical remedies could not relieve, he had invented a theory of the human organism to explain his case, and from it derived new surgical techniques.

He describes the origin of the theory in his one prodigious treatise. The work opens with a humble declaration of intent:

"Either men will think that the nature of toothache is wholly mysterious and incomprehensible, or that a man like myself, who has suffered from it thirty-six years, must be of a slow and sluggish disposition not to have discovered more respecting the nature and treatment of a disease so peculiarly his own. Be this as it may, I will give a bona fide account of what I know."

Dri then relates how, refusing extraction, he had lost so much strength through his chronic ailment that he had at last taken to his bed, spending four months in strict immobility. ("Movement," he writes, "is one of the greatest troubles in toothache, since, with perfect quiet, the agony is just tolerable.") It was thus bedridden that Dri began speaking to his teeth, at first cursing them, then praying to them, finally addressing them as sensible beings in need of consolation and reassurance. A prompt diminution of pain followed Dri's first essay in "internal charity." Three days later several afflicted teeth, including the one first smitten thirty-six years before, stopped aching. Only two refused to be comforted. After another week of encouragement, the doctor decided that they knew themselves unfit for life in his body, wished to be free of it, but were unwilling to take the initiative of leaving him. Dri patiently assuaged

their anxiety, explaining that there was only one escape
from their predicament, and that by delaying to choose it
they were aggravating their suffering, not to mention his
own. In a week, without being touched, the reluctant teeth
fell out.

King Dri's conclusion from his experiment might be
summarized thus:

The human body, richest of nature's fruits, is not a single
organism made of constituent parts, but an assemblage of
entities on whose voluntary collaboration the functioning
of the whole depends. "The body is analogous to a political
confederation, not to a *federation* as is normally supposed." Every entity within the body is endowed with its
own psyche, more or less developed in awareness and self-
consciousness. Aching teeth can be compared to tempera-
mental six-year-old children, an impotent penis to an adoles-
cent girl who must be cajoled out of her sulkiness. The
most developed entity is the heart, which does not govern
the body but presides over it with loving persuasiveness,
like an experienced but still vigorous father at the center
of a household of relatives and pets. Health exists when
the various entities are happy, for they then perform their
roles properly and co-operate with one another. Disease
appears when some member of the organism rejects its
vocation. Medicine intervenes to bring the wayward member back to its place in the body's society. At best the
heart makes its own medicine, convincing the rebel of its
love by addressing it sympathetically; but a doctor is often
needed to abet the communion of heart and member,
and sometimes, when the patient has surrendered to uncon-
sciousness or despair, to speak for the heart itself.

In his treatise Dr. Dri gives many examples of such
intervention. The following paragraph, the close of his

plea to the infected canine of a sixteen-year-old boy, may suggest the Indian's stature.

"You say, 'Is not the goal of life to die rather than to live, not leaving death to the mercy of others but acceding to it voluntarily, and giving one's self up with rejoicing?' No! that is neither joy, nor liberty, nor grace, nor eternal life: which are in your father's love. Child of my being! Flesh of my flesh! As distant from death as the morning star is from a farm's smoky fire, when that fair virgin on the sun's breast lays her radiant head, may your father in his infinite love behold you forever in that place reserved for you! Next to such life, what is death worth? And what is life worth if not given to him? Must you torment yourself, when obedience is so sweet? Return and say: 'Now I have all! Everything is at my feet, I am as one who, on seeing a tree laden with fruit, and having mounted the ladder, feels a depth of branches bend under his body. I shall speak beneath the tree, as a flute neither too grave nor too shrill. Behold, I am lifted upon the waters! Love unseals the rock of my heart! So let me live! Let me grow thus mingled with my father, like the vine with the olive tree.'" The tooth was cured.

The medical profession had not taken R. King Dri seriously during his lifetime, despite the attractiveness of his theory and the undeniable results he achieved in Punjab dental wards. According to Dr. Zarater, however, a new interest in the philosopher-dentist had arisen in Europe, and a movement was under way to establish legal recognition of his teaching.

During eight months as Dr. Zarater's assistant, I learned the clinical uses of King Dri's theory, as well as the rudiments of traditional dentistry. Under the directress' guidance I made such progress that, after only four months' training, I was able to treat simple cases by myself. And no sooner had I taken on this responsibility than a valuable patient was assigned to me.

I had hoped to benefit from my position. As the clinic ministered to the entire camp, I would inevitably meet members of sects other than my own. But I was lucky that one of the first of these should be a young Fideist woman named Yana, celebrated throughout Jacksongrad for her beauty; more pertinently, Evelyn Roak was in love with her.

In order to see her often, I prolonged Yana's treatment. I also wooed her myself. (Dear Yana! I became devoted to her. Even when she had lost her usefulness, I remained her friend.)

My courtship was successful. Yana and I began meeting secretly in a storeroom of the clinic. We were obliged to address each other by gesture or in writing, for Yana spoke no English, although she had learned to read and write it in school. An unexpected result of this was that we invented a written code in the course of our exchanges. The code was then only a game between us; later, when we had to rely on letters, it became a valuable safeguard.

I was passionate with Yana but unpossessive—I had no wish to anger her Fideist suitor, for whom I feigned admiration. (Lest this arouse suspicion, I asked Yana not to mention my name. "A dangerous political matter," I explained.)

Meanwhile I had Yana deliver to her Fideist friend a succession of anonymous gifts, most of them articles then scarce in the camp—absorbent cotton, airmail stationery, Swiss toothpaste.

Six of the presents were innocuous. The seventh and last was a pound box of caramel candies. I had cooked them myself and mixed into them several ounces of crys-

talline oxylous acid. Normally inactive, this chemical com-
bines with certain phosphates into volatile compounds;
their formation requires no catalysts other than moisture
and mild heat.

I expected the stickiness of the candies to attach a quantity of acid crystals to the teeth, where they would trans-
form the calcium phosphate of the enamel into oxyluric
acid, a violently corrosive substance.

Four days after delivering my present, Yana told me
that her friend was ill. I mounted a sleepless watch at
the clinic entrance. Early the next morning the patient
was brought in on a stretcher and taken, as I had ordered,
to my office. But Dr. Zarater had observed the arrival.
It was she who conducted the examination, and she decided to handle the case herself.

"These cavities," she exclaimed, "are *monstrous* and
unnatural!"

Yana's admirer proved generous—eight other Fideists
later called at the clinic with stricken mouths. Even Yana,
unwarned, lost a molar.

The Infection

Dr. Zarater had good reason to keep me from "my" patient.

My severed fingers had healed with difficulty—even healed, they remained abnormally sensitive. Recently a few pimples had appeared on the stumps, adding to their soreness a tormenting itch.

The pimples were small, lying nearly flush with the skin, with minute white spots at the center. I forced myself not to scratch them in the hope that they would soon vanish, and I would have left them untreated if Dr. Zarater had not intervened. She forbade me to touch her patients and ordered me to go to the infirmary. I neglected to do so; the directress became increasingly urgent; when she finally showed signs of anger, I obeyed.

The camp doctor was named Amset. He was a popular figure in Jacksongrad, celebrated for his addiction to whisky, monologue and fresh air. On fair days he received his patients in his garden behind the clinic, and it was there that I found him on the morning of my visit. Dr. Amset had just dismissed a patient when I arrived.

"Yes, there's little doubt but what it's cystic fibrosis!
It's a strange disease! Or if you prefer, 'familial steator-
rhea.' I like to give at least two names to things, especially
diseases and plants, which I have a grim time grasping,
memorywise. If you know that neurasthenia is the English
malady, St.-John's-wort is Klamath weed, old-man's-
beard . . . Hm—your hand! That's funny—did you—
let's see, you're a dental assistant. Wait a minute." He
sharply pinched one of the more swollen pimples; yellow
matter issued. "Did you happen to treat a young boy
called . . . called . . . a Resurrectionist I think—Moe
Kusa, that's the name! You did? Oh oh—you can call it
lues if you want, but in four other letters it's syph. It has
to be. You see, I remember Moe's mother—his older
brother was congenitally syphilitic, and Moe . . . as you
say, the sores on his mouth. Well, I'll give you three zillion
units today and gone tomorrow."

Two crows that had been circling above us settled in an
alder nearby. The doctor's cure was useless. The gamut
of antibiotics, exhausted during the wicked aftermath of
my operation, had nearly killed me. Dr. Amset agreed
there was no chance of their helping now. Pouring each
of us a tumbler of whisky, he prepared some mercurous
acetate for local application, and wished me luck.

Leaving, I thought of little Moe Kusa. He was a
charming boy who suffered his condition without com-
plaint: the ends of his mouth were ulcerated, so that
eating and drinking were painful to him, and his pretty
face marred. He was wasted too by chronic diarrhea;
and while his greater affliction was beyond my competence,
I had been able to soothe the lesser one with a broth of
what Dr. Amset might call starwort.

In the Barracks

Our quarters were cleaned and supervised by an unami-able person known as "The Concierge." Although a pris-oner, she was dependent on the authorities for her privi-leged job, and she accordingly acted in their interests rather than ours. Her role was contemptible, but I took a tolerant view of it—a minor power, she was very well informed.

For a long time I could not persuade The Concierge to trust me. My assignment to the clinic seemed of little use, since she had incorruptible teeth and perquisites greater than my own; yet it was through my position that I at last won her over.

The Concierge's joy was her pet, a miniature urubu. She spoiled it elaborately, nursing it through the ordeal of the Jacksongrad winter and providing it in all seasons, to our dismay, with gamy morsels of animal brain and eye. The vulture was as little liked as its mistress, and a re-sentful prisoner finally kidnaped it one night while The Concierge slept, returning it before dawn with its beak smashed.

Unable to pick or chew, the bird starved. The Concierge was in despair, and herself wasting away, when I intervened. Retrieving two wisdom teeth from the clinic, I fashioned out of them a dentine beak, cut away the ruined bills and wired the new ones to their roots. After a few days the urubu began using the substitute, soon mastered it, and quickly recovered.

The Concierge was "at my service." I made her promise to tell me immediately, no matter how great the difficulty, any news she might hear concerning the Fideists.

Wandering into the barracks one Sunday morning, I found The Concierge alone, reading a back issue of *The Worm Runners Digest* and listening to the radio. An English-language program was being broadcast—

> *the people themselves*
> *terrible spider plague?*
> *the webs upon*
> *more like tents than*
> *wind*
> *than German incendiary*
> *a decoration*
> *"food rose plants" from light and air.   citizens*
> *the autonomous   Joe, the natural*
> *penis?*
> *the phoenix*
> *sprays   dust*
> *ravaging*
> *Then in your view, Greg, a giant smoke screen has been spread between the facts of medicine in America*

"Those shmucks have muff it again," The Concierge remarked, switching off the radio to answer the telephone.

"This is Calvin nine oh nine oh." She listened a moment and hung up. "I think that soon, very soon, I have important news." She smiled horribly, and turned away to begin her weekly cleaning. A duster of which she was very proud (but which she never used, as the asthma faction was apt to remind her) hung from one shoulder. It had been made from the hair of Laris Kotinskaya, a Hollywood actress who, having to shave her head for a prison role, had given away her locks in response to The Concierge's distant appeal. No one knew why she had turned the trophy into a domestic implement.

Texts True and False

Dr. Zarater reduced my position at the clinic to that of accountant; my baseball stratagem failed; and I despaired of exploiting legitimate opportunities. I felt that I must find a lure attractive enough to justify a secret meeting.

I knew that Evelyn Roak was something of a dilettante (as children, we had studied music together), with a flair for history. According to Yana, this interest had recently led to a study of the sects represented in the camp, particularly of Darbyism and its origins.

This news left me perplexed until I remembered the "Black Pope" enigma.

The rise of Darbyism is plainly told in contemporary documents, all of which are published, and all but one easily accounted for. The exception is as mysterious as the rest are clear. It is an unsigned letter of about seven hundred words, composed in a farrago of tongues; no one has yet identified or explained it. Scholars refer to it as *Pape Niger*, after its opening words.*

It was my guess, which Yana confirmed, that her friend's interest in Darbyism centered on this letter.

Using Yana as intermediary, I therefore let it be known

* See Figures 1(a) and 1(b) for the version of the letter that appeared in *Notes & Queries*, Vol. 2, No. 3.

that I too was interested in *Pape Niger;* that I had access
to a document bearing on the Darbyist letter in the Defective Baptist archives; and that I had made a copy of it.
To support my fiction, I forged a short "extract," adorned
it with pseudo-scholarly notes, and gave it to Yana to
show to her friend.

I enjoy rereading my invention. Its tangential relation
to *Pape Niger,* offering little to satisfy but enough to excite an expectant curiosity; the mystifying notes, in which
slivers of apt information are sandwiched between thick
irrelevancies; the interruption of the text at the point when
it evidently becomes most interesting; and above all the
presumption that *Pape Niger* was addressed to one of
the Allants in an attempt to denigrate the Catholic Chavenders and their allies, while the Defective Baptists tried to
pacify the warring families—these devices seem now no
less cunning than they did when I put all my passion into
them.

Here is what I wrote.

The history of the Chavenders and the Allants is truly
of the heroic nobility: a stock of peculiar strength, whence
sprung great trees, and from the trees, great fruit.

Gloomy are these days of drooping gray fears among
the golden-haired Chavenders. There is now much stored-
up pain among the volatile Allants; and from this place I
have heard the heavy din of verbal doughtiness. When
Chavenders meet with Allants, there are swelling looks and
injurious words, and many times brawls between them, in
our day; but in the historicity[1] of the clans is kinship and
assurance. Here is the piety of family life, here is the
sanctity of family religion where we may not look for
other.

Two and a half centuries ago they united in wedlock:
Doña Enula de Osorio, (by her sister) a near Chinchon,

PAPE NIGER jets ricovra su podestoir, und stes assedut en les moutoncillos tuskanos dispergent sos magias super i juices d'ogne part, grosse ubre de porco mal. E in tua dolor uoudriestassais tu, mee framano, an unam suam pezonaro noero chuper. Attunzione! Els von te dammamnerum, quel rasse sempere paranda amb faulsschid di destruir. Custodissent Darby, Irving, autorque *Pulsuum Compendii* te a illoris, lles demons: le sun toto porcherie. Nel ano domini nostri 1632 beporcten li Europa, e tost muorons por lor mjerde. "Niente plas coctura di melon, niente plus coloquintida, ningente plu huole de rizino! Fellate solo an bonam viellam chinchonam, la pulvem comitissae," oder plutost pelvem comitissae, com lor? E quando sa lor le caldepisse donato habue, ed un schankro belo suppurantem, fact qualgue lor dammé legne? No, mesmo se la de qual juide De Vega (*sic*) por 100 reals per lb. pris avan!

Comprendo tua angunia. Escrivs, "This molar continues to grow both in heighth and breadth, I cannot close my jaw, which is become unhinged, and has given me such fevers that my bed every night is drenched with sweat." Ma ne empla quela scortecha! No ave lors schankrs guarit—y qual a? Mercur purgo lo porcherie per lor annoigrato esput. Desempacha tò ventre delo ecxesifo de corrupouriccio que tu en ti oltre los besognes des fams encogt as, und la doulour y fievras s'en despedirano con lu. Lo Pape Niger no post la facre, toddo pourchoriture lu stesmo. Prov nigrum helleboro —qual es, com Sanct Polo dique, "escandal pour les Juides y follocurie per les pagans, ma pouter de Diu por los que aclamati son" —e se lo purgase demas étrenuif fuss, allievile abhec cet vin: "Five spoonfuls are to be taken every morning and at five p.m. ℞ Peony-root, Elecampane, Masterwort, Angelica, aa ℥j; Rue-leaves, Sage, Betony, Germander, White Horehound, Tops of lesser centaury, of each a handful; Juniper-berries, 3 vj; Peel of two oranges. Slice, and steep in six pints of Canary wine. Strain, and lay by for use." Lo pancho va se no solament quiete facer, ma tu poras to purificazion maintener, en la corrumpcion copiusament forpissans.

Car sais que l'heor proxima es. Diu va les mortos giustos en par-

Fig. 1 (a)

fectes cuorpos ricompor; ma li vifs deuren suos propruos cuerps parfar cor por els van les juzés; per aquest scribe S. Pollo, "Ne scabez-vos que vestro corp lo timplum des Sancti Sprit sai?" Da purgati; und durant tu deglutis, di "Huat hana huat ista pista sista domina damnaustra luxato."

Et se nosaltres dobram nos purifiguer, mi frare, besogne per natturalas mezias ser. Queli sales e solutiones quemics di quale parlas —i son sol magie de strujas vestuta como scientie. Ne suivir Dr. Theophrastus Bombastus Malatastus Heresiastus Catastrastus! Ma sechurament ç'a no perigolo de quel-la. Aquell uomb fo un so patidifus, e suon gran Mysterium es uno vaporetto (ich meine, ein kleiner Mist!). O sents tu com un peddo de insalato staño? Pensis tu che la vecinanze d'un chaldo fuoc te in uno maron malolorodoriferante pozzanguère e una blu flama trasformerà? E fan les estrelles tu chabelli plu prest croiscents, y t'adormen le marees, y te reveigle un terretremblor in Paraguay amb un irisistible pet in Hannover? Quant a "tartar" e "Diathesis exsudativus"—a lui mas un esciancro curat?

O, es tut aus Trotula, aquela affar; lla es mare de tutos nostros mals, y la corrozio que nos spuerc. Sapiens matrona davveritude!—piu tost putens latrina, y Odoricus ava un odor muy ricco quand su nom ses labres paseron—bocapudre! Ellas son tute poipas de caca, e nos nascions embarbrouillats con esa. La sola passio de cête mulier fu ses chancres con fards de coubrir, y su nos de braguegar! No es en tele compagnia que nos deveniam limpidos—"car il tiene que aquest corroptible corp la incorruptibilida rivest."

Adeu, mio frallo, soy de buon cor, rencendre tu spe. Tant bien, escris su ta ganasch cis paraules, "✠ Rex, ✠ Pax, ✠ Nax in Christo filio," e si secur, subretot pendent el son, d'un convenebol color d'estre cingt. Mi amor e abec toi en cet exhortation, e ie prec Deu nos de permetre nos vientost de rancontre. Aci il fa bel, et le vin de ceste anee sera bon—si nos beurons le temps où il vut sara. Ie me subviens tout le temps de cet apareill extravagant avec les ampoules qui ilumine votre lit, cet un obget que l'on parfois à la campagne sortir debrai pour qu'il verd comme une rosse devieng.

Fig. 1(b)

who married into the Allants by the help of the selfsame
Del Vega[2], bore an amiable sturdy daughter, a little bro-
ken-headed, her part good partly violent nature had been
distempered (as many of their unquiet climbing spirits)
in Paracelsus's school of healing; but this was a future vir-
tue.[3] Entering the medical service, she had met and la-
bored with a Chavender youth, in a terrible pestilence, in
Genoa, where they were both infected. Afterward, the
familial ires spent, they married in England, and settled
near London, attaching themselves to the fortunes of Hector Chavender, from whom they obtained a worthy station.

Many are the examples of Chavenders, in subsequent
times, attaining by the exertions of their sagacity, the
heights of honor: the follicular "patch" that bears their
name, Baillie's tribute, and the authoritative collaborations
of Rolando, and Kussmaul of "fearful dyspnea" fame—do
they[4] not attest it? Other is the Allants' glory: from generation to generation they ministered dangerously to the
plague-ridden; the first German dispensary for poor children was their merciful act, in Hanover; a practical keen-
ness shewed them[5], that nitrate of silver cleansed the eyes
of babes, long ere any might reason it; and one, fated to
die cruelly, has had, at last, distinguished letters.[6]

Infinite are the distempers of the human spirit, man is a
prodigy of misery, lesser Allants and Chavenders have
there been than these, on occasion. One, a century past,
butchered his mother; one his wife; another publicly corn-
holed[7] his little daughter, and was hanged; others pursued
disgrace more meanly. Over such the families have not
fought; but then such are not needed to inflame them; for
many have been the ills of others, to serve as ills of their
own.[8]

Now let them aspire &c.

(*The document concludes with a long plea to reunite the
two families in the Baptist faith.*)

1. The writer, who apparently means by this word a consciousness of genealogy, supplies matter for new discord where he hopes to reconcile. In accordance with their progressive inclination, the Chavenders have always traced their ancestry through a line of medical innovators to an origin in Trotula, of the school of Salerno; while the Hanoverian Allants, Galenists until 1700 and still conservative, claim their succession from the less notorious Salernitan Alphanus I, doubtless the person who later became Archbishop of Salerno, but not to be confused with another Archbishop of Salerno of the same name. The distinction, insisted on by both families, is petty; for in their tradition of close attendance to the patient the Allants follow the Hippocratic instruction as faithfully as the Chavenders, who are so particular to defend its theoretical consequences.

2. The implication is that Doña Ana de Osorio, the first wife of Count Chinchon, was treated with cinchona by the Count's physician Juan del Vega. Doña Ana died before her husband became Viceroy of Peru, and it was the second countess, Doña Francisca Henriquez de Rivera, whose fever was cured by the controversial bark. This was not known until the twentieth century, after the document was written.

3. Although Catholics, the Chavenders had supported Paracelsus.

4. Hector Chavender (1619–1688) discovered the aggregation of lymph nodules known as "Chavender's patch" (1660). Matthew Baillie attributed to Evelyn Chavender (1730–1781) elements of his description of lesions. Ello Chavender (1775–1851) collaborated in Rolando's investigation of the spinal cord, and Jeremy Chavender (1819–1880) in Kussmaul's research on acetone.

5. The same pragmatic instinct made Walter Allant (1818–1901) drink a pint of typhus culture to prove that typhus had a non-bacterial origin. Koch said his failure to contract the disease retarded bacteriology by a generation.

6. The reference is to Hans Bakerloo Allant (1851–1886), whose discovery of the goundou bacteria was published in 1885. In Mexico the following year, he began searching for a bacterial explanation of yellow fever. He had the bad luck to find several cases harboring both yellow fever virus and the *Leptospira* of Weil's disease. He isolated the *Leptospira*, grew a culture from it,

developed a vaccine, and having (he thought) immunized himself, proceeded to West Africa, where a yellow fever epidemic was raging. He succumbed immediately.

7. A word of unknown origin, probably from the French *encanailler*. Professor B. M. Jemm's derivation (made in discussing a contemporary instance) from *The Cornhill Magazine* seems no more than wishful thinking.

8. The writer means that the two families feuded over medical issues. For example:

Forceps Royalties. In 1699 Chubb Chavender announced the obstetrical forceps. He did not, however, describe the instrument, which had been used for several generations by his branch of the family, midwives by profession. Attempts by outsiders to learn the secret of the painsaving apparatus, whose renown attracted many women, were unavailing. When a group of civic-minded Londoners collected a purse of £500 to be bestowed on Chavender, he accepted the money, but in return gave up only one blade of the forceps. In 1725 his son, learning of the invention of another forceps in Europe, disclosed the entire instrument against a further sum and an exclusive patent.

The Allants asserted that the forceps (together with Enula's daughter) had come into Chavender hands from them, and claimed a share of the money. There was subsequently much bad blood between the two houses on this account.

Purging. Shortly after, the Chavenders attacked the Allants for their views on purging. Accepting G. E. Stahl's theories, the Allants not only purged universally but never checked the "hemorrhoidal flux," which they thought was a healthy process. Evelyn Chavender's father wrote Wilhelm Allant that "without doubt he would presently claim the title once held by the Chief Physician of the ancient Egyptians, viz. 'Shepherd of the Rectum,' except that 'butcher' might fit the truth nicer."

Bleeding. In 1810 the families corresponded abusively over the quantity of leeches used by the Allants. The latter declared it never passed two hundred a day; the Chavenders counted by the thousands. It should be remembered that at least ten Allants were practicing at the time.

The Telephone

When Yana's treatment ended, my meetings with her became difficult and infrequent. We often resorted to letters composed in the code we had invented, and it was in writing that Yana reported the effect of my counterfeit document, only a day after she had transmitted it:

spunoɯ ɯosoqun noh soom hund dood suooms X

I replied,

mous ou moʎs I oɯoʎ snoɯhuouhs sumo dood dos SI

Two days later she wrote,

uooɯ hq 6 mou mommod SOS

(SOS stood for urgency of any sort.)

Before the appointed hour that evening, armed with a hatchet, I went to the clinic storeroom that was still our meeting place. In a while Yana came, alone. The strands of hair beneath her fur cap were silvered with rime.

Conversing by gesture and code (which we spelled with our forefingers in each other's palm), I learned that a summons from the camp authorities had detained Yana's admirer, who had asked her to arrange another meeting.

Stupefied by disappointment, I said nothing. After a long silence the telephone rang. I lifted the receiver and heard a muffled voice ask, "Is this Luther one six six oh?"

"No, Melancthon one eight eight six." (It was really a Loyola number; these were passwords.)

In a more natural tone The Concierge continued, "The sugars are selling the shop to Moscow. Five of them out tonight: La Rouille, Prizon, Donders, Valsalva, Roak."

I managed to tell Yana the news. She was surprised and happy—she would now be wholly mine.

In the following weeks the guards became laxer in their supervision and we were able to meet more easily. I afterward found out that Yana and I had been peculiarly favored. We were on the point of being disciplined when the intelligence service intervened and requested the camp authorities to tolerate our relationship. The reason was their interest in our code. They had intercepted our letters but could not decipher them, although they hoped to do so with more material. Their leniency worked against them: the guards extended it to our rendezvous, our correspondence dwindled, and the code remained unbroken. It would have vexed the local cryptologists to learn there was no true cipher, only simple inversion.

Three and a half years before in the Breton town of Roscoff, the chef of La Sole Retrouvée, distractedly mistaking a bottle of maple syrup for Calvados, used it in a sauce for broiled lobster. The dish thus invented became popular in Paris the following winter, and it started a vogue for the syrup that in less than a year spread throughout Western Europe.

A report of this reached Jacksongrad in a radio broadcast denouncing the fashion as an example of Western degeneracy. It occurred to an observant inmate of the camp that a nearby maple forest might provide syrup for the new market. The trees having been tested and shown to yield a rich sap, a group of Fideists set up an organization for tapping and refining the virgin store. The camp authorities, eager to find occupations for their wards, approved the initiative and supplied labor for it. They also turned a blind eye on the disposal of the produce, except for a quantity of sugar requisitioned for camp use.

Because of the remoteness of Jacksongrad and the criminal status of the entrepreneurs, marketing the Siberian syrup was a formidable task; nevertheless the Fideists, efficient, imaginative and unscrupulous, soon showed a profit.

Their chief problem was getting the syrup to Europe at a feasible cost. Careful planning with collaborators outside the camp led to the following solution.

Initially, the merchandise moved by rail: south from Jacksongrad on the Chkalov-Tashkent line to its junction at Ursat'yevskaya with the Andizhan-Krasnovodsk line, on which it traveled westward as far as Tedzhen. The organization paid the railroad the preferential rate accorded camp manufactures.

From Tedzhen camels carried the syrup to Meshed in Iran, via the valleys of the Hari Rud and Kashaf Rud. This route had been an empty return for caravans, and the drivers did the work cheaply.

At Meshed, terminus of the railroad south, the syrup was loaded into three ancient oil cars leased from the Iranian government. The price was low, and the organization made agreement to a long-term contract contingent on a rebate in freight charges. Thus, at minimal cost, the merchandise reached Bandar Abbas on the Persian Gulf.

From there to Marseilles, transport was provided by Ulek, Manis & Petis, a Macao firm with a branch in Hong Kong.

The effectiveness in the treatment of baldness and impotence of the old Chinese "jissom cocktail" called *hui tê* had recently won it a following in Mediterranean Europe. As it was known to contain arsenic and glass splinters, its legal entry was everywhere forbidden, but enthusiasts still bought it on the black market for as much as two hundred dollars a pound.

Ulek, Manis & Petis were the principal dealers in this concoction. Since it was plentiful in Hong Kong, where it entered from the mainland, they had no problem of supply. However, they had long been dissatisfied with their European outlets—UMP used established smuggling agencies, which are notoriously conservative and would handle only a small fraction of what the market demanded. They had decided to distribute *hui tê* themselves when, through intermediaries in Peking and Semipalatinsk, the Jacksongrad organization approached them with a request to import maple syrup.

Recognizing an excellent cover for their *hui tê* trade, the Macao firm accepted the job at once. The importers would ship and market the syrup, underwrite all initial costs and provide many secondary services. In return they asked only a small commission to be collected as a percentage of sales.

With the consent of the Fideist group, Ulek, Manis & Petis set to work.

First, they contracted in Hong Kong for the manufacture of syrup containers—cylindrical tin cans attractively papered with red, white and blue labels. Some of the cans were constructed to hold a secret quantity of *hui tê*. A diaphragm of soft alloy, parallel to the end of every such can, divided it into two compartments: a large upper one, to be filled with syrup blended with a potent *hui tê* solvent; and a small lower one in which *hui tê* concentrate was tightly packed. When opened, the top of the can disclosed what seemed to be ordinary syrup. Opening the bottom, which was reinforced with steel, demanded a pressure great enough to force the compact *hui tê* against the alloy diaphragm and break it, thus mixing the extract with its solvent and instantly forming a liquid undistinguishable from the syrup by sight or taste.

Outwardly all the cans were alike. Those without *hui tê* were made heavier to avoid a discrepancy in weight.

A UMP ship brought the cans to Bandar Abbas, where they were filled; and thence to Marseilles. The entire cargo entered France as syrup, Ulek, Manis & Petis paying the duty on it. A transport concern owned by the company then took charge of the shipment, which was sorted in the privacy of its trucks and barges. The syrup mixed with solvent was thrown away, and the *hui tê* repackaged for delivery to specialized middlemen. The pure syrup was entrusted to normal marketing channels.

Success attended the international ruse in all its stages, and the two enterprises flourished. The availability of *hui tê* maintained its popularity and won it new adepts. Because of its quality and cheapness, "Mabel's" became the household word for syrup from Ulster to Anatolia.

At the end of a year the Jacksongrad group paid its debts to Ulek, Manis & Petis, thereafter investing its profits in that company. After the second year, the prisoners' interests were nationalized. The government's aim in this was not so much to recuperate private wealth as to control the disruption of the American syrup trade. In exchange for ownership, the prisoners were given their freedom and appointed to run the business as Soviet officials.

These Fideist prisoners, the "Sugars," were the five whose release The Concierge announced to me over the telephone.

Dhaversac

If this event crippled my hopes, it only strengthened my will, and I decided that in the new circumstances I must try to escape.

On the long train ride to Jacksongrad I had become friends with a fellow Baptist called Robin Marr. The friendship had already proved useful. Robin was a first cousin of Yana's, and very intimate with her despite their sectarian differences; so that when I met Yana my interest in her seemed a natural one. A greater although heretofore neglected advantage was that eighteen months after my arrival Robin had begun preparing for escape. I had then refused to join in the attempt. I asked to participate now, and Robin, after consulting the two other partners, accepted me.

The partners were Laurence Hapi and Beverley Zuckerkandl.

A radical organ designer who had been, before imprisonment, preoccupied with difficulties of pitch control in new instruments, Zuckerkandl had experimented at the camp with an unusual mineral, a kind of apatite named after the geologist Wolff. The mineral had proved capable of solving

the problems of tuning, and Beverley was impatient to
return to Soda Springs, Idaho, and test the discovery.

Hapi, a painter of French extraction, had a quite different motive for escaping, which was once more to eat
ice cream in Venice. Laurence said to me, "The war will
blister our skins and corrupt our bones, I shall sit at Flo-
rian's still, on bare heels, with a crate for a table, *gianduja*
pressed from the brick-dust of flattened palaces, sipping
canal-water coffee, while skeletal bands wring their fiddles,
gazing on the wingless dusk," and wept.

Robin Marr planned the escape and was our unques-
tioned leader.

At my first conference with these three, I learned that
recent information had resolved the issue most keenly debated by them: what route the escape should follow.

Two months before, Moscow had ordered a double census to be taken in the more primitive regions of southern
Siberia.

Of the two purposes of the census, one was sanitary:
reports of endemic plague demanded a survey of the rat
population. The other was economic: a project was under
study to develop the area, among the poorest in the Soviet
Union, and the responsible planners wanted to find out
what kinds of livestock were best adapted to it. They
hoped subsequently to improve the more promising breeds
with technical help and public funds.

The census takers, crisscrossing the territory along a
northwest-southeast line, were to count sheep, goats and
grunting oxen on the outward leg of their journey, rats
on their return.

Unfortunately the uninformed populations misunder-
stood the survey. They thought that rather than a measure
undertaken for their well-being, it was a prelude to the
taxation or confiscation of their herds; and at the approach

of the census takers they drove their animals into the hills and hid them. It was only when the first count was virtually completed that its purpose became known. The Siberian peasantry, learning of the subsidies awaiting them if the number of their livestock was sufficiently high (but whose loss was now a certainty) were preparing to petition for a new census when they heard that the investigators were doubling back through the country. They did not know that it was for a different reason.

Since their job was to search out infection, the census takers hoped to have the least possible contact with the local populations. Instead, the peasants dogged their steps. This might have been only an inconvenience if the natives had not crowded every available farm animal into their path, and if a small fraction of the rats they were counting had not been carriers of disease. The disease was not plague, but the animal cholera known vulgarly as "bats' boils," fatal to goats and sheep and highly infectious. It followed the census takers along their thousand-mile journey at an interval of six days, in an epidemic that destroyed over eighteen thousand head of livestock before their work was forcibly stopped; that is, until a committee of angry peasants pursued, ambushed and murdered them.

Only one member of the party survived, the geographer Dhaversac. He fled the assailants on foot for eight days, and at last took refuge in our camp. Assigned to the Defective Baptist mess, he related his adventures to several prisoners there.

One of the prisoners was Beverley Zuckerkandl, who repeated Dhaversac's account to my other partners. By tracing the geographer's flight they learned that the army and police supervised the country around the camp at best haphazardly and in some places not at all. Perhaps because no escape in that direction seemed possible, the district immediately north of us was quite unguarded. This fact had almost cost Dhaversac his life; it might well save ours, and it decided the path of our escape. We would start north, then trek southeastward through a succession of mountain ranges, and finally turn east into a spur of Afghanistan. If Dhaversac's information was true, our route would be free of human obstacles.

During his few days among us, Dhaversac impressed us as intelligent and humane. He was despondent over the fate of his expedition. "We proved again, and how painfully! that mistakes in scientific procedure have inevitable social effects. A census that alters the size of the population it studies is a deadly absurdity."

"Hapi"

The rare green of a few low, precocious plants signaled the winter's end. We had planned our escape for early spring. The weather would be the mildest of the year, and our sect's fiesta, falling then, would be a fitting occasion for our attempt.

The climax of the annual Defective Baptist fiesta was a "home-made animal" race. Like the other festivities, it was held in the sports area that lay on the northeast boundary of the camp.

The race was open to the entire sect. To qualify, a contestant had to enter a racing car made according to two rules: only labor and materials available within the Baptist compound could be used, and the car had to have the shape of an animal. The contestant was free to decide what sort of motor power to install; since fuels were scarce, it was usually human muscle.

Two prizes were given at the end of the race, one for speed, one for the best design among the cars finishing. As the race was four versts long, winning even the second prize demanded mechanical skill. The prizes were generally lavish. The year before both had included twenty shares of Ulek, Manis & Petis stock.

Robin Marr saw a great opportunity for us in the coming race. We were to head north: not only was the sports area on the northern side of the camp, but no barrier separated it from the country beyond, since the grounds were kept clear for use as a landing field. As competitors, we would have access to the area equipped for our undertaking; and we could openly prepare as an entry a vehicle in which to make our escape. The chief drawback was a rule forbidding riders—it meant that during the race three passengers must be kept hidden; in other words, a provisional one-seater would have to provide camouflage for them as well as for the vehicle the four of us would later use.

The advantages plainly outweighed the difficulties. We entered the race and began constructing a suitable car.

It was designed on an extravagant scale. The visible machinery was huge—twin pulleys at the front, operated by weighty hand cranks and attached by a web of broad belts to the "rear axle." The hidden machine was an assemblage of bicycles that Beverley had stolen over the years from the Athletic Department. We originally intended to be mounted in tandem, hoping to gain speed by the low resistance of our single file. An event that preceded the fiesta by a few weeks modified our plans.

Defective Baptists, as their name suggests, perform baptism as an indirect and partial aspersion of adult members. The sect believes that man's condition is absolute imperfection. All men require baptism, none deserves it, and even those who have been baptized win only a fleeting purity, since not even divine grace can long redeem mortal corruption. Baptism must be renewed at least once a

year, and each believer must earn his right to the sacra-
ment. The sect exacts heroic feats of its adherents. In
1949 six thousand Baptists gathered near the Meije, in the
French Alps, and were directed toward the summit of that
forbidding mountain, where a helicopter had lowered a
teapot of holy water. In Jacksongrad such grandiose cere-
monies are impossible, and the Defective Baptist elders must
improvise tests of faith. The camp authorities, well aware of
the problem, let the sect use the sports area to give it a
modicum of space for its ordeals.

Twenty days before the fiesta my three partners and I,
together with the rest of our division (about three thousand), assembled in the area for the baptismal competition.

The Defective Baptist elders—the elders, whose average
age was twenty-two, were those who had obtained baptism the previous year—decreed the following ritual.

The aspirants would line up along the sides of the
sports area, while the seventy-one elders gathered in the
center. Each elder would carry in one hand a cup of holy
water and with the other lead a leashed black duck. At a
predetermined moment the elders would douse the ducks,
loose them and drive them toward the aspirants, who then
had to catch the birds before they shook the water from
their oily feathers.

The mass baptism took place on a crisp afternoon in
early March. It testified both to the fervor of our sect
and to the madness such fervor breeds. The pandemonium
of pursuer and pursued was grim to hear and see, and those
engaged risked tangible injury. To avoid suspicion, Beverley and Robin joined in the scrimmage: they were kicked
and mauled.

To the high passion for salvation, moreover, was joined
a sordid vengefulness; for one of the guards, intervening

in the rite, became the object of the crowd's ecstatic hate. Whether from the will-dissolving confusion that the spectacle provoked in him, or from the momentary rousing of an unsuspected instinct, or the resurgence of a repressed one, the guard, finding one of the sanctified birds at his feet, seized it by the neck with one hand, with the other ripped open his trouserfly, and began (adding his private folly to the hysteria around him) copulating with the glossy bird that now trumpeted in an agony of terror and perhaps pain.

In a moment the guard realized the sacrilege he had committed—a number of Baptists, black with outrage, were already charging at him. He had been standing near the edge of the sports area, and a dozen strides brought him onto the plain beyond. He began loping across it toward the mountains, with a speed all the more remarkable for the writhing bird still impaled on his sex. The baptized and unbaptized ran after him. The other guards lost five minutes restraining the mob, so that by the time they were free to pursue the renegade he had definitely outstripped them. Two tanks were dispatched, but the fugitive had gained the first gorges, about a mile away: at the foot of the mountains the tanks turned back. We were then marched off to our compound. Except for the apologies of a superior warden, we heard no more of the event.

We learned two pertinent facts from the scandal of that afternoon. The first was that other than army tanks, the authorities had no motorized means of pursuit. The second was that the tanks could not enter the mountain defiles where we hoped to follow the runaway guard. Our plans were changed accordingly. Maneuverability, not speed, was what we needed most. Since the slow-starting tanks could not catch even an unequipped fugitive, four of us pedaling

our machine would easily elude them. If, reaching the
mountains, we could then drive our velocipede a mile or
two farther, we would distance our pursuers decisively.

The tandem we had first imagined was too long for the
sharp turns of the defiles, and we therefore replaced it
with a new design rapidly conceived and executed by
Beverley. To my regret, I cannot describe that ingenious
machine. I was sworn to secrecy at the time, and I have
yet to be relieved of my oath. I shall only mention one
detail that has come to light elsewhere. The "Wolff's apatite" that Beverley had studied turned out to be a "stone"
of great elasticity. Thanks to it, the suspension of our car
had a resilience adequate to the rough terrain through
which we were to drive.

While Beverley, aided by Robin, built the mechanism of
the car, Laurence and I made the body. Our job was important. As it had to provide space for three riders as well
as the secret vehicle, our "single-seater" looked hope-
lessly large. We therefore announced that we hoped to win,
not the race, but the prize for design. It was necessary to
justify the claim.

Our contraption had the form of an oblong box. Its
volume was irreducible, and any improvement of its contours would have increased its size, so we resorted to pic-
torial decoration. The hidden machine provided one sculp-
tural touch and decided what animal should (as the rules
demanded) give our entry its "shape." Near the front of
the box, bicycle handlebars protruded. The suggestion of
horns was unmistakable, and disguising the handlebars as
such, we made our car a bull. I named it *Hapi*, in honor
of Laurence, whose wrinkled doglike face beamed at the
honor.

We decorated the four sides accordingly.

On the front we painted a stylized bull's face in massive stripes of black. Underneath it I wrote:

On the right side, we spelled out a textual maze in brilliant and varied colors. (See Figure 2.)

On the back, we drew a black diamond-shaped figure—the "grid" that, superimposed on the verbal maze, reveals its solution (Figure 3).

On the left side, we printed, in yellow and white letters on a black ground, the true text of the maze:

Enter the labyrinth. After twenty steps, you must decide whether to turn left or right. In either case, follow the outside wall—the right-hand wall if you have turned right, the left-hand wall if you have turned left: that is the rule for mazes, being Ariadne's thread without the spinning. You walk, in either case, on a black tile floor, down a crooked corridor, along a twelve-foot-high wall of smooth yellowish stone; but if you have turned left, each section of wall, between the first and fifth corners, is pierced with circular windows two feet across, through which you may regard, should you so wish, four landscapes outside the labyrinth—perhaps alders against the sun; campers gathered in front of their tents in strict meditation; three bundles of cut branches piled together; or a thrush singing, although you cannot hear him through the leaded window, on a

marsh plant. If you have turned right, as if in compensa-
tion various pictures, words and emblems are soon figured
on the corners of the blind wall you follow—more precisely, on the concave section of wall that forms the
corner's outer side, and one at every corner until the
eighteenth. At the fourth corner you may see a bark toss-
ing on stormy blue water; at the next, a pugnacious bust
of Julius Caesar; next, the card symbol *spade* repeated
three times; then the Greek army marching in convex pat-
terns before Troy besieged; the letter *delta;* four spade
symbols; a map of the southeastern states of America, in
white paint; the word "Amen," incomplete, drawn in capi-
tal letters across a setting sun; four more spades; a drop
of some black liquid, painted much larger than the spades
but resembling them; and last (but singly, one to a corner)
four spades. Under all these images runs a continuous sequence of words printed in two superposed bands of which
each is the reverse of the other. The eighteenth corner,
like the seventeenth, is blank. The wall into which it leads
has a small circular window through which you can see
a mimic thrush, and similar windows in each of the next
three walls reveal views of firewood, campers and four
silhouetted alders; while if you have, on entering, turned
left, you will encounter at the second corner after the
fourth window (the fifth in all), above a repeated punning
sequence, a spade, followed at each successive corner until
the twentieth by a spade, a spade, another spade, an en-
larged drop, four spades, an AMEN, a map, four more
spades, *delta,* the Greek army before Troy, three spades,
Caesar, and a bark. Then, no matter which turning you
took, and it did not matter which one you took, you will
have reached the entrance, for the labyrinth leads nowhere
but out of itself.

with a
  thread out the mimic
    Ariadne's spinning thrush
      being delta perceive you singing
        mazes which on
          3 bundles rule for through a
            of cut the letter then dow circu-marsh
              branches is of small plant
                piled left: that the America 4 spade has a
                  together: turned in eastern it leads
                    firewood have white the south symbols which
          if you paint map of into
        left wall then a wall Entrance out of
          wall—the the word a spade 4 more but the Enter
            outside an AMEN each is a spades blank labyrinth
              follow the incomplete of which al of the is after
                stone in bands and other 18th cor 20 paces
                  yellowish capital superposed emblems runs a the you
                    smooth letters in two are words punning sequence must
                      some printed soon pictures like the decide
                        of drawn images fig if right 17th whether to
                          wall across all these right turn

                  the under on the or

                        Greek a setting blind bark left
                          foot army sun a spade wall a tossing if left
                            twelve before you follow see on stormy each
                          along a Troy spades at the may blue water section
                        besieged four 4th at the of wall
                      ridor Troy corner larger then a between the
                    crooked before a than much pugnac first
                  campers down a patterns then to the painted bust corner
                gathered tile floor convex in one spades liquid of Julius is pierced
              in front black army marching singly next black Caesar with
            of their on a army some at last the
                        tents in you walk Greek another drop of the the circular
                          strict perhaps the more de-enlarged card windows four alders
                        meditation perhaps an symbol two silhouetted
                      —spades of a spade feet against
                  yrinth repeated across the
                the lab three 3 through sun
              outside times which you
            spades may regard
          landscapes should you
    50
4 wish

Fig. 2

NOTE. The publisher regrets that Fig. 2 has been incorrectly set. The shape of the text should conform to that of Fig. 3.

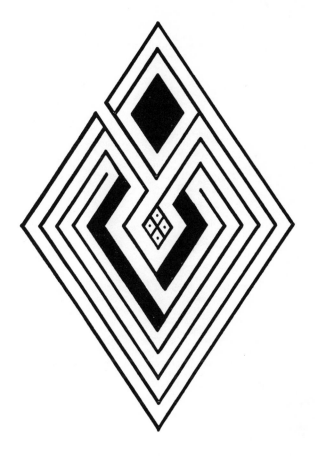

Fig. 3

The Fiesta

The race took place on the afternoon of the first Sunday in spring. All through the previous week Defective Baptists were seen gazing southward, as if expecting a portent. On Friday morning they were given satisfaction. About twenty miles south of the camp eight hills dented the horizon: they now seemed to emit a puce-colored cloud which, low-lying and dense, slightly blurred their contour.

The cloud suggested earthquake or war, but was due to a struggle for survival in the arachnid world.

Wolf spiders (I believe the variety has never been classified) infest the southern hills. They resemble the *Lycosa opifex* of the steppes, living in subterranean nests with trap-door entrances. The winter leaves these nests in a precarious state. Frost and drought have turned the earth to dust, and until the late spring rains restore its adhesiveness it gives the spiders scant protection. Moreover the end of winter exposes the spiders to their worst enemy, a small migrant chough that flies north in great numbers at the equinox. The chough prizes the Jacksongrad spiders and will dig them skillfully out of their crumbling lairs.

Against this danger the wolf spiders have created a communal defense.

In the last days of winter the spider population starts spinning thousands upon thousands of little silk bags, which look like gas-lamp mantles, but are of a tighter mesh. Each bag is packed with bits of friable earth and then sealed.

An open forest of ash trees covers the spiders' territory. The filled bags are carried by the insects into the trees and hung along their boughs, until every branch and twig more than five yards from the ground is clustered with them—"the image," Laurence told me, "of a marshmallow bonanza."

The choughs fly north on the first south wind of spring. At its rising the wind blows high, leaving an uneasy stillness at ground level that persists for a day or two. It is during this time that the choughs appear. When the high wind starts, the spiders, waiting on the branches of the ash trees, cut the strands that attach the laden bags. Falling to the ground, the bags disintegrate in puffs of dust. Within minutes innumerable tiny explosions gather into an unfathomable cloud. The spiders return to their nests, hidden from the choughs' keen sight. The dust screen does not usually settle until the birds have flown past.

Each year the Defective Baptists watched anxiously for the spiders' cloud; for the south wind which it heralded was considered propitious for their rites, and one ceremony materially depended on it.

On Friday afternoon centuries of choughs chattered over our camp; on the ground the air remained still. Saturday brought the first flurries of warmth. By Sunday the south wind blew through Jacksongrad unabated.

The morning of the holiday was spent by the sect in private prayer and thanksgiving. Toward noon, among the other race contestants, we trundled our car to the sports area.

After a light meal (the heavy eating was reserved for supper), the Defective Baptists walked in a loose body through the camp, showered in every compound with brickbats and jeers. At the sports area they deployed for the ritual concert that would open the public festivities.

Of all the traditions of the Jacksongrad Baptists, the concert was the most esteemed and the most painstakingly observed.

It had begun more than a hundred years earlier, at the original location of the camp. Since then, each year had added to its grandeur and its fame. Inspired by returning prisoners, Baptist communities emulated it the world over, but never with much success, for the spectacular performances of the camp were beyond imitation. The annual event in the end remained a local glory.

Six generations of prisoners had inherited, enriched and bequeathed the collection of instruments with which the concert was performed; it now numbered a thousand and ninety-eight. The variety of the instruments was extraordinary, but more remarkable was their common attribute —they were all made from the human body. A single fact will prove the enthusiasm of our sect for the concert. The only parts of a Defective Baptist that were ever buried were the musculature and a few soft organs. The rest were used to build new instruments or repair old ones, a custom that partially explains why the Darbyists and Resurrectionists so despised us.

The instruments had other peculiarities. They produced single tones. To be played, they were set in a strong current of air, which would of itself excite their strings or air columns. Hence the concern of the Baptists with the south wind: without it, the concert could not take place.

As individual musicians could at best perform isolated notes, an exact communal discipline was needed to combine them into music. This pleased our ethical wardens.

At the time of the first concert, a learned prisoner had tuned the instruments in the Aeolian mode, and the key was piously observed.

The wind that afternoon blew with comforting force. Since the music to be performed was antiphonal, the Baptists were ranged in two equal sections facing each other. The sections were equipped with identical groups of instruments. Roughly half of these were "strings" and half pipes. The former resembled monochordal lyres of many sizes (some of the smaller ones had several strings of identical length). Their frames were made of flat or thin bones —shoulder blades, hipbones and sacra, single or joined; strands of nerve, skin, gut or wound hair were stretched between their extremities. The pipes were hollowed round bones of every size, from pierced teeth to femurs sawn and mounted in sixteen-foot columns. The largest instruments of each type needed squads of prisoners to handle them.

A smaller division of instruments was percussive. It included arm bones against which the wind blew light phalanges (stuffed so that they would not themselves resound); tarsal rattles; bladders inflated and dried, in which one or more teeth had been confined, whose clattering produced sounds of definite pitch when the wind swung the sacs; and skulls, with wings of skin on metacarpal frames to catch the wind, containing shriveled eyes, similarly swung.

Smallest of all was the group of sympathetic instruments, intermittently used for color: skulls and hardened bags of membrane, from which nearby music would elicit a faint hum or whine, as well as chord-producing assemblages—

the only exceptions to the monotonic rule—of mixed bones and fibers, both natural (a child's rib cage) and artificial ("Salome").

When performers and instruments were symmetrically aligned, those of us exempted from the concert—elders and race contestants—gathered in the space between them into a large square. The center of the square was a knoll about three feet high, made for the occasion out of roughly piled damp clay. An old prisoner, who had performed the office for twenty-seven years, mounted this uneasy podium to conduct the concert, at once raising a hand (in which a short charred object served as baton) to demand the attention of the multitudes on either side. They fell silent, and for a while we heard only the steady sighing of the wind. Then, at the fall of their leader's hand, the bank of musicians that faced the spring sun sounded the opening A-minor chord of Racquet's *Pia Mater*.

I shall not forget that music. Anxiety for what the afternoon would bring may have magnified my feelings, but there was a beauty in the spectacle beyond its effect. With a deliberateness imposed by physical circumstance, grave phrases of lapidary simplicity were exchanged by the twin assemblies. Where on one side a choir of white flutes was thrust up into eerie shrillness, on the other, stretched ranks of glistening multicolored tissue and hair answered with a melancholy twang. I have heard no organ, orchestra or electronic device, nor any aboriginal combination of gourd and drum that produced so rich and unfamiliar a sound; and the timbre of the instruments, and the massive mechanical gestures with which they were played, were peculiarly fitting to the music, whose measured diatonic chords and tune were unadorned to the point of bareness, but filled with the archaic fervor of Huguenot piety.

As I listened and watched, unexpected grief over-

whelmed me. In sudden terror I apprehended my separa-
tion from those around me, and from the abandoned hopes
of my childhood—I had perhaps revered them too much,
and now they disgusted me. To steady myself, I squeezed
the silver medal I always carried in my right pocket (it
was so worn from touching that the inscription *Violon,
1ᵉʳ Prix* had become illegible); nevertheless I wept. One
of my neighbors, also weeping, then caught me by the arm
and exclaimed, "It is like Beethoven's *Erotica!*" My sobs
kept me from dealing violently with the intruder. Afterward I was thankful that my self-indulgence had been cut
short.

The race followed the concert. That morning we had
lined up the cars at their starting positions in a corner of
the sports area, on whose perimeter the course lay. Drivers
and their teams now gave their entries a last inspection.
The entire Defective Baptist throng followed us to examine the cars, which numbered forty-four in all. *Hapi*
attracted a large group that speculated on our designs and
inscriptions, especially the maze on the tail.

"I couldn't get to first base."

"*C'est comme quoi—une grille de mots croisés?*"

"For a funfair, it isn't much fun."

Screened by these onlookers, my three partners pretended to tinker with the car. One by one they slid beneath it and climbed to their hiding places—narrow platforms equipped with foot braces and grips, on which they
would sit until we cast *Hapi*'s shell. I had been picked to
drive because, as the largest, I would have been most difficult to fit inside.

The crowd withdrew to the center of the grounds.
When spectators and contestants were in place, my clear
view of the track discovered only two guards.

With a wave of the arm and a cry of "Milton!" the

erstwhile concert leader started the race. I could see but not hear the word, which the south wind, rising still, carried downfield.

I lunged against *Hapi*'s two hand-cranks. My hidden companions, whose position allowed each to push one of the three cumbrous wooden wheels that bore our visible car, helped at first, then properly reserved their strength.

The racecourse was a rectangle less than a mile long and half as wide. Starting north at the southeast corner of the track, contestants had to drive once around it, finishing where they began (a fact alluded to in our maze). We had only to complete one leg of the race and, at the first corner, continue straight over the plain.

I had thus to propel *Hapi* for about sixteen hundred yards. The machine worked with a lumbering inefficiency that would have left us conspicuously far behind had not the greatest drawback of the car, its bulk, turned to our advantage: it offered so broad a surface to the following wind that our speed was doubled and we were able to keep up with a few less agile competitors.

This led to a singular stroke of luck.

Eight minutes' labor had winded me by the time we reached the northeast corner. Before the turn I had drawn even with another entry, which was now straining ahead on my left: *Ergo,* a squat but majestically antlered stag. *Ergo* was the only machine in the race with an internal combustion engine. As fuel it burned the rubbish used to light the heaters in sentry boxes—half-consumed bits of oil-soaked rag, hoarded during two winters. So far it had performed erratically, its abrupt sprints declining noisily into spells of immobility. Now, as it passed us, *Ergo* disappeared in the whish of a mild explosion that filled the air with a cloud of greasy blacklets.

The cloud not only engulfed our car and hid us, it gave

us an excuse to lose our way. Cranking with new vigor, I
directed *Hapi* toward the open plain. When I reached clear
air, I looked back. *Ergo* was a dim heap in the middle of
the track. One of the guards was running toward it, ges-
ticulating. I saw to my surprise that (evidently in fear of
another explosion) he was waving us onto the plain.

The moment had come to bring forth our velocipede.
I shouted to my partners to wait and help me increase our
speed—

"They're still in the dark!"

We struggled on for a minute, gaining a hundred yards
for all our clumsiness.

Then, leaping from my seat, I struck four rapid blows
on *Hapi*'s flank. At the signal, my companions drew the
bolts that held the frame together, and we quickly dis-
engaged the skeletal machine within. In half a minute we
were on our saddles, pedaling hard (I, after my exertions,
somewhat inadequately). The mountains rose before us in
a splendor of afternoon sun, matching our hope.

Another minute passed before the first tank started in
pursuit. Behind us the dusty ground swarmed with white
snakes startled by our passage. We were eight hundred
yards ahead of the tanks when we reached the mountains.

We entered a narrow gorge and followed it at top speed
for half a mile. Laurence then collapsed with abdominal
cramp. We stopped to rest; in a few minutes the pain subsided. Resuming our advance at a moderate rate, which
the twisting ascent of the path further slowed, we covered
another six miles in the next hour, at which point our
vehicle succumbed to the terrain, breaking an axle. We
unloaded our packs and set off on foot. There was no
need to hide the wrecked machine. The sheer-sided gorge
left no doubt as to our direction.

Soon afterward the full moon appeared to the north, in

the strip of sky above us. Daylight was waning, and the moon shone overhead with deepening golden warmth until a turning in the gorge obscured it. I can remember nothing of the landscape but the alternating earth and rock under my feet as the path steepened.

For three hours we hiked with only momentary rests, taking turns in the lead to keep a steady pace. Just at sunset, we reached the top of a cliff that overlooked the Jacksongrad plain. A tiny column of soldiers could be seen marching toward us—our last glimpse of Russian authority.

Around eight-thirty we stopped on a small plateau below a pass to eat and rest. The moon, now fiercely bright in the dark sky, cast a stern gray glow on the fields around us. We considered sleeping there, but Robin, uneasy, moved us on.

Crossing the pass, we descended a steep gulley, and at ten o'clock, staggering and numbed, settled in a grove of silver firs. The air was bearably cold, but for some time I shivered with exhaustion and relief. We drank at a nearby spring, set out our bedding on the soft ground, and soon fell asleep.

As I lay wrapped in the folds of my blanket, I saw the moon return among the crags to the west, and heard Beverley salute it drowsily: "Sister, good night!"

Part Two

Zuck

I have forgotten much of our journey. Particular days and hours have accumulated into generalities of exertion and rest from which they can no longer be recovered. Fortunately Robin Marr kept a log, and I have used it to fill out my account.

The first day was fair. We changed our northerly course in mid-morning and turned southeast, following the hills beyond the first mountains. On our left, to the northeast, lay a valley about five miles broad, divided by a winding river at which the undulating prairie below us ended in precipitous masses of rose-colored clay. Across the valley was another range, where, Robin noted, a *white streak of limestone is discernible. Over this a bright green ribbon, a brown stripe above; then peaks (snow).*

Later: *a small oblong-shaped range.*

In the afternoon we descended to a much lower altitude to cross a tributary of the river, filled with spring thaw. We found a bridge, two juniper trunks laid over the stream, with smaller logs athwart them. There was a confused distribution of shrubs here, already budding. Robin mentions *Inula helenium.*

Climbing higher (height gave at least an illusion of safety), we overlooked, in a widening of the valley, a vast network of *aryks* or irrigation canals. They spread out like a spider web from the quiet, smoky village at their center.

We ate frugally but pleasantly that night, around a small fire kindled in a hollow of the mountain forest.

Zuck: organ.

I was only half-awake during Beverley's description of the planned instrument, but I shall try to expand Robin's notes.

Blackblende. This highly elastic material was to be the main component of the organ pipes. Thanks to black-blende, the mouths and bodies of each pipe could instantaneously expand or contract to any size. The substance can easily be regulated by electrochemical means: through a system of electrical impulses, Beverley could make one pipe rapidly perform a succession of distinct notes—in other words, if only one part were played on it, a single pipe could replace an organ rank. (*For coupling, counterpoint &c. 4 per rank.*)

Blackblende is as volatile as it is elastic, and before coming to Jacksongrad Beverley had not found a way of controlling it. Mixed with blackblende, apatite would check its volatility without impairing its usefulness. *Indifferent to weather (organ bane ever).*

Swell as pipes: the swell box, made of the same mixture, would have great "expressive" power.

Fletcher's trolley without Reynolds' number! I cannot explain this.

Skimpy porcupine at distance—because the pipes, few in number, were to project from a sphere containing the performer. *Near, lively multiple bubblegum. Gripping obscenity of science fiction. Zuck perhaps kidding. Or*

*manic upswing? Krampoez mad? So early—too. All organ
fiends fiends.*

Delivered with hypnotic enthusiasm, Beverley's account
convinced me I was sunk in a despondent baroque hallucination. The fire seemed more exotic than the imagined
instrument.

Burning mountain. Ignition of carboniferous layer. Although this note ends Robin's entry for the day, I am
sure we saw no such thing. The night was clear, with a
plenitude of stars.

Spires and Squares

During a pause in our march, we took turns observing, through Beverley's binoculars, a village lying on the valley floor below us. A wall of gray mud enclosed a few dozen dispersed houses. Small gardens, each with several trees, adjoined them. Outside the wall, meadows of alfalfa stretched to the foothills through scattered willow copses. The trees grew thicker near the river, whose swift concentrated waters blazed in the sun.

To the south, the range we had followed bore eastward, rising to considerable heights. Its peaks were sharp-pointed, or had the form of crenelated towers, with snow-covered platforms at their tops. Clouds perpetually gathered and disintegrated about the summits. There was also snow on the *counterforts*, and later in the day we saw that in the upper parts of the valley its whiteness covered much of the spurs separating the transverse gorges. Before reaching that colder region, we turned southwest through a pass *perhaps thirty-five hundred feet* high. Soon after, we came on an alpine lake, five miles long, more than half of it covered by dun fur-tipped reeds; it contained an abundance of leeches.

The southern slope of the range was warmer and greener. Mountain grasses grew thick upon it, and the junipers yielded at a higher altitude to birch and ash, through which flourished an undergrowth of black-currant bushes and mountain *emula*. We advanced along a series of easy ridges. Another valley appeared on our right. *Hills of drift—clay and boulders.*

We pitched camp. Laurence vanished and returned presently with a large bird. No one asked how it had been killed, but I guessed that it was found dead. We roasted the bird and ate it. After two days of dried rations, the taste of fresh food exhilarated.

That evening Robin Marr recounted an autobiographical episode.

"I spent most of my last year at college preparing my bachelor's thesis. Research often took me to the university library, and I soon began spending most of my time there, not unhappily for one as addicted to books as I am. One day, while browsing in the stacks, I spotted Frost's *Lives of Eminent Christians*. It was a book I had never seen, and being something of a Butlerian, I took it down at once. The copy was new, not even cut; but into it someone had slipped a sheet of fine paper, on which a few words had been written in careful, old-fashioned script.

"Although the words were simple, their arrangement was baffling. At the top of the page three letters set one above another formed the Latin

r

e

s

Beneath them, there were three deliberately incomplete sentences:

> The Mother cannot —— her Son.
> The Son —— his Father.
> The Mother —— their Spirit.

The initial letters of *mother, son, father* and *spirit*, originally written small, had been obliterated with heavy capitals. Near the bottom of the page, well separated from the sentences, was a phrase of German, penciled lightly by the same hand:

Zwei Herzen in Dreivierteltakt

"I sorted the paper among my notes. Coming across it a day or two later, I considered it at leisure.

"At first glance I had taken it for a student squib whose blanks stood for common obscenities. The third sentence now seemed to belie this impression—even the possibility of a decent conundrum was spoiled by the gravity of *Spirit*.

"I put the paper away and for a while forgot about it.

"In the spring I finished my thesis. Before beginning work on it, I had sometimes published informal essays in the college magazine; the editors now urged me to contribute again. Looking for a subject, I remembered the enigmatic paper and decided that it might serve as a pretext for a few pages of chatty prose.

"My essay was dull, but it had an interesting effect on me. I began by describing the paper and my discovery of it, and observed that the simplest words were sometimes enough to reveal the depth of our ignorance. The statements on the paper, for instance, at once reminded us how much we had forgotten of the Holy Family, in spite of long years of religious schooling. A bland sentiment—yet even as I wrote, I began suspecting that theology, which I had (I thought) invoked arbitrarily, might well be the sub-

ject of the incompleted sentences. By the time I finished, I
was convinced that their one purpose was to raise doctrinal
issues in the reader's mind. The capitalization of the nouns
was the only proof of my conviction; yet the sentences began turning in my brain, quickening a relentless curiosity
about 'the divine nature.' What extraordinary acts and es-
sences in the holy relationship had been reckoned in three
gnomic sentences that evoked, more tellingly than chapters
of definition, the intricacy of supernatural being? In what
way was, and was not, the Mother a mother, the Father a
father, the Son a son? My essay ended on a dissatisfied note
—I could not hide my feelings entirely and did not dare
expose them with unfashionable reflections on the Trinity.

"Privately, I determined to find out what the sentences
meant. It would take time, but knowing this was itself
an advantage, for impatience in solving riddles often over-
looks what is plain in its quest for the mysterious. I set
aside an hour or two every day for an unhurried investigation of the problem.

"If I told you the details of my search, we would be
up all night." Beverley and Laurence were already asleep.
"I must have tried to fill the blanks with every verb in
English. But I shall spare you the catalogue of my mistakes.

"I soon learned that no one word fitted all three sentences. Many worked in two but proved weak or in-
consistent in the third (for example, such verbs as *blind*
and *peruse*). Experiment also showed that while two or
three unrelated words might give a sensible reading, they
hardly crystallized the dogma that I felt must underlie
the sentences and make of them one statement rather than
three.

"From the start I had read the letters standing above
the sentences as the Latin *res*, here denoting *matter* or

subject. It occurred to me that the letters might be a clue to the missing words. I tested this hypothesis; and after wasting time on verbs beginning with *r, e* and *s,* I found a 'true' solution. Three different words filled the blanks. Each began and ended with the letters r-e-s, except for the one in the first sentence (which, since it described imperfection, was properly imperfect). Best of all, the solution made absolute sense.

"The words were *resire(s), restores, respires.*

"To show why this choice satisfied me, I must go a step further. In writing down my solutions, I always listed the words in a column. I noticed that the middle sections of the words beginning and ending in *res* formed another column that sometimes had a meaning of its own. In the final one, for example—"

Robin scribbled on a slip of paper and handed it to me. I read:

res	I	res
res	to	res
res	pi	res

"The non-*res* letters made *I to pi.* This seemed a clear if laconic reference to the doctrine that I thought the three sentences expressed, and I supposed that *res* had been written vertically to draw attention to it.

"By the way, my work was not entirely private. My collegiate essay on the 'res paper,' as it came to be known, had elicited interest . . ."

I began to doze.

". . . a major influence in not to drop . . . mode cut off a little review. I was printed notes . . . stone accounts of my efforts. A small-key reputation. Persuasion? minor forged several articles 'New factors in the res paper Enigma'—pity"

(For a moment I fell asleep. I dreamt that the four of us were gathered by Beverley's new organ. The instrument was built of luminous materials, copper and studded leather, that softened the effect of its terrific armament of tubes. Beverley was playing, accompanying the brightness of my violin with muffled chords. Robin and Laurence stood near us, listening and shadowy. My left hand was restored; we played some sweet *settecento* work. Sometimes the music altered to a sound of distant shrieking.)

". . . entertaining hoaxes . . . explain the *I to pi* syllables: the Itopis, a race of Indians living in 'the extremity of Idaho,' were Christian before the arrival of whites . . . But these 'con' versions . . . —advertised by booksellers at silly prices.

"To return to the three sentences.

"One of the subjects most passionately debated in the early church was the nature of Christ's divinity. Could God be made, or remade, in a mortal's womb? Could God be both god and man at once? Nestorius, the fifth-century patriarch of Constantinople, devoted his life to defending his views on the question, saw them accepted by the church, but himself suffered degradation and banishment. In his old age he wrote *The Bazaar of Heraclides of Damascus*, in which he cleared himself brilliantly of the charge of 'Nestorianism,' and defined his doctrine. 'In the Person,' he wrote, 'the natures use their properties mutually. The manhood is the person of the Godhead, and the Godhead is the person of the manhood.' The Word passed through the Virgin Mary, it was not born of her; the body was born of her and received the word: 'of the two natures there was a union.' The union is and shall always remain an ineffable mystery; it cannot be doubted.

"Consider my sentences in the light of these ideas. 'The Mother cannot resire her Son': eternity cannot happen twice, and the male word *resire*, ironically applied to the Virgin, underscores the impossibility. 'The Son restores his Father': after His passage through the flesh, God is still whole. 'The Mother respires their Spirit': the Word, like air, has moved through her, but is not of her.

"Now imagine God, in medieval fashion, as a perfect circle. Assume that the center of the circle is a point representing God as man, God having taken on the minuteness of an identity, of an 'I.' You know that a straight line connecting the center of a circle to its circumference is a radius; that two opposite radii form a diameter; and that division of the circumference by the diameter yields the number *pi*. Isn't *pi* then a just symbol of the Holy Spirit, by Whom the mystical union of God and man is accomplished? Doesn't this give the syllabic formula a fitting sense? *I to pi:* the man becoming Spirit, and so remaining god?

"One day, almost three years after discovering the 'res paper,' I had my theories confirmed—and destroyed.

"It was midwinter. I was lying in bed with the flu, expecting my doctor, when the morning mail arrived. With it came a letter from an Englishman who knew my articles. He wrote to tell me that he had found, in the last edition of Edward Davies' *Celtic Researches*, mention of a sixteenth-century Latin translation of the *Bazaar of Heraclides*. Davies reprinted, as evidence for some delusion of his own, a typographical ornament from the translation. This is how it looked."

Robin carefully drew a diagram:

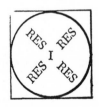

"My correspondent made some interesting comments on his discovery.

"He was sure that 'I' in the illustration was the Roman numeral one. The author of my sentences had adroitly changed or expanded its meaning by placing it in an English context.

"Second, he suggested a connection between *I to pi* and Euler's equation.

"Next, he observed that the square around the circle implied a fourth word, *resquares*, or in Latin, *res qua res*, 'the thing as thing,' 'the very reality,' and could itself form a square:

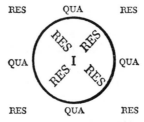

"Finally he chided me for ignoring the German words penciled below the sentences. Apparently trivial, they referred without doubt to the hypostatic union. The 'two hearts' were the two natures of God, human and divine. They were 'in three-quarter time' because they were joined in the consubstantial union of the Trinity, which formed a single perfect measure. (The *triple* meter was crucial here, but my correspondent added that *quarter*-time might symbolize the square.)

"The letter gave me irrepressible pleasure; only the abjection of fever kept me still. The doctor arrived. She examined me, confined me to bed, suggested aspirin and liquid diet, and prescribed an expectorant for my cough. Her prescription read:

M. inf. 3 f3 pulv. inulæ in qt. aq. Sum. q. i. d.
Netsonoff

"I glanced at the cryptic notation. The initial M was peculiarly written, three vertical strokes capped with a flourish. It resembled the M of 'Mother' in the res paper. I looked farther. Was it fact or fever that discovered a similarity between the 3 of 'f3' and the Z of 'Zwei,' or the S's of 'Son' and '*Sum.*'? With foreboding I asked Dr. Netsonoff to wait while, over her protests, I got up and fetched the original document from my study.

"Confronted with it, the doctor identified the writing as her own.

" 'It's a first-year German exercise,' she explained. 'The sentences were originally in German and had to be completed with particular verb forms. I must have translated them as a first step. How funny leaving them in the stacks!'

" 'What about the capitals?'

" 'I don't know—perhaps I was trying out German usage in English.'

" 'And *Zwei Herzen* . . . ?'

" 'Sometimes we sang German songs in class—it was a summer course. This is the title of one.'

" 'And *res?*'

" 'That's the way the three German articles are abbreviated, by their last letters—*deR, diE, daS.* Did you notice it spells the Latin word for "thing"? Now get back into bed.'

"So that was it—*res qua res.*"

Robin stirred the dying fire. I was soon asleep in the cold night.

Dol

Excellent condition: we cover much ground. The next morning came to a flat & barren watershed, with a similar slope declining southward. Aryks are few, only on their fringes a bright verdure, reeds and wild lucerne. Between the canals a marl steppe, a gray parched soil, with poor vegetation, withered wormwood & sickly bushes of Ephedra. The valley was devoid of meadowland, encumbered with boulders, amongst them the river flows in divergent streams, shallow and now quick. A cluster of felt kibitkas, & cattle enclosures (why here?) made of heaped brush. We rounded east—through by noon, over easy hills.

Beyond, a rich valley—west of passage, what seemed wheat, melon patches. The river woodless except for planted white willows and poplars.

Black steppe under high mountains. Waterless springs; scanty wormwood, elecampane. Tiring day through hollows, gulleys; time lost. 20 miles. At sunset, ascent through masses of micous schist. Junipers—among them, v. high, camped. The pass still higher—ca. 7000 ft., visible over us.

Laurence told us:

"After the war, I spent several years visiting the Mediterranean coasts of Spain and Greece, settling nowhere, moving from one village to the next at intervals of a few weeks. I began painting again, in a new style. Painters saw and encouraged my work, and occasionally I found a buyer in the expatriate colonies I visited.

"In 1953 I returned to Paris. It was there, shortly after my second exhibition at a little gallery in the Passage du Caire, that my fame began. Esberi, the Parisian critic, published a book of articles on contemporary art called *Magic Moments*. A single page was devoted to me, but it was the most flattering one in the book. He wrote: 'Hapi's abstractions are simple, subtle and overwhelming. They remind us that art at its highest is not removed from life, but is its master. In these small, poignant works, line no longer articulates the mere surface of the painting, but reinvests the whole visible world with contours of mythopœic beauty. Their sense of space expands about them so richly that the solar system becomes intimate, and the interval between man and man a cosmic tragedy. As befits a master painter, Hapi's colors are most exciting of all; after them, the universe enters a new and unsuspected season. What is one to say of the extraordinary blue that figures in each of this artist's works? I have never seen anything like it, and I am forced to conclude that Hapi's genius is chemical as well as painterly. Be that as it may, the blue—sometimes only a dot, sometimes extending over half the painting—seems always to function as beginning and end, and it runs through the corpus of the work like a mystical, personal leitmotif. But it is more than personal. Indeed Hapi's blue should end all discussion about the realism of abstract painting. With a precision Van Eyck would have envied, it denotes unfailingly that everlasting focus of our nostalgia for a golden age of classical purity—the serene, exalted *azur* of the Lesbian sky.'

"I remember the passage exactly because it changed my life. It was true that the blue in my paintings was their 'point'; once this had been demonstrated, their charm became apparent to anyone who took the trouble to look at them. My success was complete. My next show sold out before it opened. I was given liberal contracts by galleries in New York, Paris and Maastricht, and my financial boom had its critical counterpart. By the end of another year my paintings were in such demand that they vanished into the selling circuit. Dealers outbid the richest collectors in the certainty of reselling at a still higher price, and my works traveled from gallery to gallery, rarely stopping long enough even to be shown.

"Critics, collectors, dealers, all agreed that the outstanding characteristic of my work was this *blue*. You can imagine how unhappy I was to have my art reduced to a single device, to have the work of years swept away in a flood of misguided praise. What most infuriated me was that my admirers believed the effect of my blue to be inherent, when it depended on the interplay of all the colors used; the blue itself varied slightly from painting to painting.

"I tried to make this clear to those who could have understood me and who should have been readier to do so. It was a useless effort. People admire luck, not labor, and I was confined to the role of prodigy.

"There was only one course open to me. In solitude and anguish (for I loved my blue world) I worked out a new method of composition, which I revealed at a well-publicized show in New York.

"I not only expected failure, I counted on it to free me from the stereotype of my success. But my failure was of another kind.

"Reaction to the exhibition was summed up at the opening by an anonymous lady in furs who declared, embracing me, 'Darling, you *are* a genius! No blue in the paintings, and yet one is aware of nothing else. It is sublime.'

"Shortly after this I turned actively to left-wing politics, and so came to Jacksongrad. Believe me, it was a change for the better."

When Laurence had finished, Robin asked me to speak about my past life. I followed the example of my friends and limited myself to a professional anecdote—my laughable attempt to play the violin left-handed.

Abisnaya

The pass below which we had camped introduced us to a cold plateau, where for two days we suffered from our lack of shelter; winter still prevailed there.

Our progress was helped by a natural phenomenon in the high gorges we had to cross. Masses of snow accumulate on the cliffs of the gorges during the winter and at springtime tumble down into them. The torrent at the bottom washes out a passage for itself in the heaped snow but leaves a permanent unmelting arch above it. Since the sun hardly penetrates the narrow chasms, and since the avalanches fall every year in the same places, high snow bridges build up between the gorge walls. They spared us laborious climbs and removed altogether the problem of fording the rapid streams.

We recovered a temperate altitude with relief. A pleasant sight heralded the change—an unbroken carpet of forget-me-nots mantling a vista of gently descending slopes. We came to a valley that was extensively cultivated (*wheat, cotton*) and by-passed it to the east. By doing so after dark we avoided returning to any notable height. Laurence, however, fell into an *aryk*.

The next steppe looked rough from a distance but offered no difficulties. Its most remarkable feature was a mold that blackened vast tracts of its yellowish soil. Robin believed it to be the residue of vanished forest. *Soil later became greenish marly mud.*

We crossed a range of mountains so low as to be under the timber line. Animal life was abundant—badger, wild boar, and many birds. We killed several huge partridges. Beverley observed that when frightened they invariably ran uphill through the brush-filled gulleys. It was easy catching them, one of us beating the gulleys while the others waited higher up with blankets and sticks. The largest bird weighed fifteen pounds.

Strange sandstone formations, caves and rain-deformed rocks, were common. Among the many plants and trees, Robin notes hawthorne and Lady-Helen's-tears.

At dawn on the morning of April 6, a shrill racket woke us. When our first panic had subsided, we recognized the noise as music—whistles and flutes, and men chanting in a high register. In the twilight we distinguished a group of thirty figures gathered above our camp. As we got to our feet, eight of them left the others and walked down toward us. They were dressed in pale billowing *chapâns* and baggy pantaloons. All halted a few yards away except one, a handsome bearded youth who stepped forward and curtsied to us. To our amazement he then addressed us in English, speaking percussively over the music:

"The Karith kings welcome you to Abisnaya.
We have descended the hills that you might be welcome.
Strangers, these boys are each a king,
As I am:
Malek Yukkhana,
Whose kingdom is Qara-Kithay, vaster than Ind.
My seventy-two provinces bind the beasts of the universe,

Camels and crocodiles, dromedaries and ephelants,
Metacollinarum, cametennus, tensevetes, alligators,
Lions red, lions white, white bears,
Mosquitoes, tigers, hyenas,
Wild oxes, wild horses, wild asses,
Wild men—one-eyed men, three-eyed men, horned men,
Pygmies, giants, centaurs; and women thus.
Alexander sired my race and locked up the beasts in its charge.
That is all.
God causeth us a complexion of color between black and
　　　　yellow, but our hearts are bright.

"The Karith kings welcome you to Abisnaya.
We have descended the hills that you might be welcome.
Next is Unc, ruler of Crit,
Kingdom of animal purity.
Does snake, toad or clamorous frog,
Does scorpion or bug
Breathe? Not there, nor does the vegetation
Suffer blame, poison-free, digestible,
And the solitary milk-and-honey plant sweet.
God causeth us to be meager, but our souls swell.

"The Karith kings welcome you to Abisnaya.
We have descended the hills that you might be welcome.
Wife of Unc, Uncia rules Mecrit.
Stones of colored clarity abound by her,
Sapphires, sardels,
Beryls and carbuncles,
Emeralds. And there also
Grows the aciduous plant, demonbane,
And pepper. Are the stars more numerous than her
　　　　　　pepperfields?
The spring of Eden Rock gushes in her court,
Its taste changing with the hour,
And nearby the sand sea stretches, waterless, rich in fish,
Which the rock river waters (for in it, rocks flow down).

Alexander, fathering Uncia's race, decreed,
'Only a woman shall rule Mecrit.'*
God causeth us to be distorted, but our tongues are straight.

"The Karith kings welcome you to Abisnaya.
We have descended the hills that you might be welcome.
Like the four winds, four brothers are kings.
        To the north rules Touschy-Talgon.
Rich, yea richer than Uncia's, are the gems of his kingdom,
But cast in the depths of subterranean rivers,
Where breathless boys, expert, mine even for days.
Touschy-Talgon rules to the north.
        To the east rules Nūshy-Thayfou.
Thou must bow, Nouschy.
He has confined the Jews in a place called Zone
Where they tailor gorgeous salamander-cloth.
Who shall tell the wonder of his cross-factory?
He is rich but modest:
Nouschy-Thayfou rules to the east.
        To the south rules Nūssy-Thâyghir,
His folk so honest, that if one lie, he die.
There are the Tomb of Daniel, the purple fish,
And the royal palace—the Palace of the Horn of the Horned
                Snake! Haha!
Nousy-Thâyghir rules to the south.
        To the west rules Nūssy-Thâyghda.
In his court a mirror stands;
There Nousy reads what passeth
In his kingdom, and beyond.
Nousy-Thâyghda rules to the west.
God causeth us an hard skin, but mercifulness.
God causeth us eminent veins, but humility.
God causeth us an hairy body, but meekness.
God causeth us small eyes, but we shall behold Him.

    *A virile beard grew from Uncia's face.

"The Karith kings welcome you to Abisnaya.
We have descended the hills that you might be welcome.
Strangers, last of our kings, consider George.
(God causeth us eyebrows joined together yet we shall all be
            saved.)"

George stepped forward and spoke in a halting voice:
"Now we eat you."

Malek Yukkhana corrected him, "No, George—now
we eat *with* you."

Still playing, the musicians descended from their post
and surrounded us. Two kings took each of us by the
hand, and in slow procession we climbed the mountain-
side.

In twenty minutes we came to a tiny village. It con-
sisted of a few dirty tents and some mud huts with a
dozen goats and sheep inside. We entered one of the tents
and were served a meal. The main dish was only *balamyk*,
rather stale. In a corner of the tent a crow shattered our
attempts at conversation with its repeated cry: "Téotoko-
toko!"

Later Malek Yukkhana took us to see their church,
where he was priest. It was a mud chapel, very much
restored but apparently ancient. Above the stone altar we
distinguished a grotesque crucifix in the gray light. Three
wooden sculptures were fastened to it on a single thick
bolt: a black child, a tall old man, and a lifesize dove,
once white. Malek Yukkhana explained that these were
movable figures of the Trinity, and that each took yearly
turns "on top" of the others. The Son was then foremost,
the Holy Ghost (almost out of sight) against the cross.

We bought a felt tent or *yurta* from the tribe, washing
it that very day in a clear brook. It proved a sovereign
protection in the heights through which we had yet to
pass.

The Mothers of the Sun

*Bustard in the meadows, sand grouse on the neighboring
steppe; along the river, geese and snipe abound. Zuck saw
foxes also. The river: lagoons of nearly still water linked
by quick noiseless currents. West, sandstone strata crop
out above the drift.*

Another day we skirted the plain of X, with *fields of
wheat and millet. Along irrigation trenches flourished
white hollyhock and the blue chicory plant.* But we kept
away from the valleys, in mountains that have resolved into
a general recollection. Their northern slopes were indented
with defiles and well watered. At a distance they had a
soft dappled appearance, the dark green of the white pine
woods blotting the bright variegated grasses. The mountain ash was their only deciduous tree, but the shrubs were
many: barberry, honeysuckle, dogberry, horseheal, wild
rose.

The southern slopes were steep, smooth and bare, with
infrequent springs.

We encountered another tribe on April 23. It occupied
a lonely plateau exposed to the south wind. The high land
had a desert look.

We needed rest, and decided that if the inhabitants were willing, we would stop there a week. Robin, who knew Uzbek, found some *manaps* of the tribe who spoke the language and with them arranged for our reception. We were given a slate hut and invited to share the communal meals.

Although their heads were of the general Kirghiz type, with gable-shaped skulls towering toward the crown, our hosts were better-looking than the natives of the adjoining regions. Their most striking characteristic was an absence of youth—they were all either children or old people. We thought at first that the harsh climate must exhaust them prematurely, but learned that their peculiar division into the extremes of age was a consequence of superstition.

The tribe, whose name meant "Mothers of the Sun," believed that the normal succession of days depended on the will of a remote, omnipotent god. Each sunrise followed on his particular command, and to be persuaded to utter it he required adoration and sacrifice. Should the worship offered him ever fail, he would unhesitatingly withhold his favor, the sun would be stayed in its subterranean cavity and the earth doomed to eternal night.

Every evening the tribe offered up to the god, in a fervent ritual of propitiation, the life of one of its members; and since the quality of the victim was thought to influence the coming day, the strongest and handsomest were always chosen to be killed.

The practice had ravished the tribe of its young men and women and was bringing it to extinction. Robin deduced from what the *manaps* said that their people, of whom there were now several hundred, had been numbered by tens of thousands only a few generations ago.

Through Robin we tried to convince the elders of their delusion. We pleaded for a simple experiment: to omit the sacrifice for one night, so that the following sunrise could demonstrate the fabulousness of their belief.

The elders were indignant. Our experiment, they said, would be criminal as well as foolish. Would we, to test a possibility, risk destroying humanity? Daily since the beginning of time the efficacy of the sacrifices had been proved—could we deny that after each of them the sun had risen?

There was no answering such argument; we had to tolerate seven murders. To mark their success, an elder every morning sported a blood-stained eyeball on the collar of his robe.

I think that if our condition had been better, we would ourselves have been sacrificed. But our shabby clothing and scrawniness spared us the grisly honor.

The Casualty

Calamity nevertheless awaited us among the Mothers of the Sun.

On the morning of May 1, we found Laurence Hapi doubled up in pain among scattered blankets. Pale, shaking with fever, Laurence motioned us to draw near and said, "Touch my belly—but gently; no, on the right." The skin was loose, the muscle beneath like a hawser.

"Perhaps—"

"It's my appendix. This is the worst of several attacks. O Zanipolo! Do you remember the cramp pedaling? That was the first. If only it wasn't me—I mean, I saw it done a lot in the Pacific, I could manage. But neither of you . . . ?"

Beverley and Robin shook their heads. (They knew about my infection, which disqualified me, to my relief.)

"I must lie quiet here. Get something to prop up my head and shoulders. Nothing to eat, but a little water from time to time."

Robin left to speak to the tribal elders, while Beverley and I stayed with Laurence, giving such reassurance as we could.

After an hour Robin came back carrying a small basket. In it were several hundred green thorns.

"Ever see these?" Robin asked Laurence, who turned with a groan to look at them. "Junkie stuff—a sort of morphine substitute."

Laurence's eyes widened. "'Hugger udders'?" Robin nodded. "Let's try one."

"I'll do it." Robin pricked one of the thorns into the little finger of Laurence's left hand.

While waiting for the effect, Robin turned to Beverley and me:

"The plant was discovered a few years ago in the Hoggar, which has a climate similar to this. The sap in the thorns is a powerful narcotic. Dope addicts in the States use them—they pretend they're toothpicks and jab their gums with them."

Prodding the flesh around the inserted thorn, Laurence said, "It works. It's terrific."

"Let me try the operation," Robin said. "There's no need to do it fast. I can follow your instructions."

"*I'm* going to try it," Laurence snapped, adding with a shrill laugh, "I wouldn't let you girls put your hands inside *me*."

We argued vehemently against the absurd proposal, but Laurence was inflexible. The issue was finally this: the patient would operate, or no one would.

Laurence slept for two hours. During that time we set water to boil and immersed in it our much-honed knives, our one needle, strips of cloth and thread, and several clamps improvised from the buckles of belts and sacks; and fitfully polished and repolished Beverley's pocket mirror.

Laurence woke up, drank some water, and decided to begin the operation at once, while the light was strong.

The first stages went well. Laurence worked quickly and cunningly, opening a delicate slit in each layer of skin, membrane and muscle as it was anesthetized by a new ring of thorns. There was little blood.

But after about twenty minutes, Laurence's gestures became reluctant and vague. We pressed our encouragement, for the moment was critical. A loop of small intestine was exposed, and Laurence held the knife reserved for the infected part. The patient's movements then stopped entirely. Laurence's head lolled; behind drooping lids, the eyes sagged.

Robin pinched Laurence's cheek and spoke sharply: "Idiot! You've used too much. Stay awake! Finish first."

The response was violent and futile. Laurence's head jerked clumsily forward and the clutched knife fell past our wary hands into the open belly, from which bright blood welled abruptly. Laurence groaned and sank back, with closed eyes. Death was quick, but irresistible sleep quicker still.

Later, several elders inquired after our friend, whose body we showed them. To our surprise, they decided that day to forgo their bloody propitiation. They perhaps did so because they themselves used the thorns to prepare their victims. Having been ritually executed, Laurence was an acceptable sacrifice.

Through the night we watched in turn over the corpse, which we had stripped and wound in a shroud of clean lint. Beverley discovered a tattoo on the right shoulder that none of us had ever seen:

Before daybreak we packed our belongings and carried the body to the tribe's sacred ground. In accordance with their custom we could not bury it, but were obliged to abandon it to weather and carrion birds. We laid the corpse in a sloping meadow as the first glow of dawn tempered the darkness. Above us, on the ridge that overlooked the fields of their dead, all the Mothers of the Sun had gathered. They stood facing eastward, their gaze fixed on the waxing day.

We left in a cold rain that washed the plateau in gentle gloom.

The Last Tribe

Below the plateau we entered low, rolling country, through which we journeyed several days. There was little vegetation, only tall tufts of a kind of vetch. The waters of rain and thaw crossed the yellow land in myriad shallow streams. After the first day, sun of summer power slowed us with unexpected heat.

We had almost crossed through this region to the next range, when, in the hot silence of early afternoon, a group of forty horsemen intercepted us. They carried various arms—lances, scimitars, carbines—and waved them menacingly.

They did not attack but halted in a circle around us. Some drew from their packs lavender-colored parasols, which they raised delicately over their heads. Others opened bottles of mineral water and swigged from them.

After a while the man who was their leader trotted up to us, rolling his eyes and growling. Having reined his horse, he gravely spread the folds of his *chapân* to expose a mighty, hairless torso. A complacent smile replaced his glower; he then tensed himself with great effort, holding his breath, making the veins on his bald head bulge in

shiny relief. In a moment his chest began to swell monu-
mentally at either side, as if balloons were being blown up
under his skin. Within a few minutes his trunk had doubled
in volume.

The other horsemen meanwhile observed us keenly, evidently watching for signs of our astonishment and submis-
sion. Beverley, prey to giggles, hid behind Robin.

Opening my penknife, I quickly took the few steps separating me from the chief and punctured his left side. The
skin collapsed with a blubbery whistle. He cried out in
dismay, wheeled his horse about, and kicking it to a gallop
rode off eastward, his men following at a desultory canter.

Robin notes that the tribe resembles *the "Narsi flatu-
rales" described by Constantine Coprogenetes,* who visited
Central Asia in the twelfth century.

We were once again in mountainous country. The first
peaks lay beneath the snow line. The vegetation was poor;
in the shingle near the summits there were examples of
miniature saxifrage, *Schultzia crinita* and other mountain
flora.

One day we crossed a *daba* caravan bound for Tash-
kent from whom we obtained information and a little
food.

That night we camped by a lake. *To the NW, low equi-
distant ridges of green porphyry radiate from the slopes,
terminating in picturesque promontories among its waters.
The shores and the lake bottom close to them are covered
with pebbles, beyond which is a yellowish clay. The one
bird seen was perhaps a widgeon; the only fishes, silverlings
and crucians. The lake is reedless; stinkfinger grows in the
surrounding fields down to its edge; starwort above.*

In the morning we met an Arab traveler who said his
name was Tham Duli. He carried a box labeled *Elisha
Perkins' Genuine Metallic Tractors,* containing two brass

valve rods. We declined to buy them. The Arab's right forearm was disfigured with a long scar running from elbow to wrist, and the fingers of his right hand moved bluntly. I remarked to my companions, "Lepromatous leprosy." The Arab shook his head, repeating the word *bajlah* while pointing at my maimed hand.

We entered higher mountains through a grand defile, whose orange-colored limestone cliffs were striped with the dark stems of white pine. Succeeding days restored to us familiar landscapes of ash, and then juniper, until we passed above the timber line altogether. In the close grass of high plateaus, among the vacant encampments to which Kirghiz herdsmen would return in midsummer, we found to our delight half-concealed specimens of alpine gentians and *Rhodiola*, already flowering. We were soon dulled by the unending contemplation of the ranges about us, packed gray masses of unvarying clay and limestone, their peaks snow-capped.

On May 13 we came upon a stone marking Grovski's skirmish of '69 (of which Robin has noted, *v.* "*Invalide Russe*"): for a day and a night the Russian lieutenant had defended himself against Kirghiz bandits behind a wall of rusk sacks.

At night there was hail.

Buffon's Ounce

The next ten days were the cruelest. We were kept at difficult altitudes, rarely less than five thousand feet, in freezing or near-freezing weather. Robin's will impelled us through wastes of stone.

May 15. . . . in the Y mountains; perpetual snows. The steeps, dry, used for pasture? No forests at all. This gives a most melancholy aspect. No minerals excepting limestone, mined in great quantities for burning, as in Dzhungarabad. . . .

May 16. . . . We crossed the first high pass—relief, but exhausted. . . . We camp at the foot of some clayey cupola-shaped eminences.

May 17. . . . dreary tableland . . .

Earlier *Zuck sighted a glacier, but I could not make it out. Detour: a mirage.* Robin insisted that in high mountains such illusions were common.

. . . in the midst of fields where only camel's-tail, our first waterless camp . . .

May 18. . . . 2nd pass—monotonous, rocks of slate and hard limestone.

Caravansary in pass, about 50 yds sq., empty. Walking

around its court, Beverley counted ninety-eight cells, I ninety-nine. We called on Robin to judge: *99 one way, 98 other; no time for discrimination.*

. . . ice in cooking utensils . . .

May 19. . . . Pik Stalina visible at est. 200 m. . . .

May 20. Approach 3rd high pass.

There, in midafternoon, a shout stopped us.

"Look!" Beverley pointed uphill.

I saw a pale spotted creature clamber catfashion over snows into the rocks.

Robin remarked, *"Una lonza leggiera e presta molto."*

Higher still we discovered the remains of an argali, or lum ox—his horns had been caught between the sides of a narrow gorge. The carcass, big as a pony's, was much devoured by birds.

May 21. . . . Z pass, last, crossed without incident . . . We descended a maze of mountain torrents.

May 22. . . . continued passage S from Z pass. Followed rivulet flowed between low hills. Gradual slope. Toward evening entered shrub zone—banks covered with tamarisk, Lycium, &c. Herbs—logocholos, with pretty black flower. Aulnay.

The night was warm, and we slept in the open. We discarded our *yurta* the next day.

May 23. . . . Valley narrowed, walls higher. We were sick of this wild scenery. At last defile turned E . . . slates prevailing . . . still gloomy . . .

May 24. . . . First tree, a poplar. It is met singly, then in groups mingled w. willow. Deep green of trees, dazzling sun—like Egypt, with sycamores for date palms. (Also NB resemblance of Kirghiz burying places to Egyptian arch.)

A little further on it became apparent we were approaching inhabited country. There were gardens, and people quietly engaged in agricultural business. We passed a mill in whose doorway two blue-clothed old men regarded us mutely over a hillock of rice.

At three in the afternoon Robin, walking about thirty yards ahead of us, stopped at the far edge of a grove we were crossing to call back,

"Alley-alley infree!"

We ran through the trees. Beyond, the ground fell sheerly to an expanse that stretched away into horizon haze: the green mustard-fields of Afghanistan.

In Afghanistan

Casting off our equipment, we scrambled down a nearby gulley to the plain.

After a half-hour's walk through thick mustard growth, we reached a dirt road. It led, a few miles farther, to a small wooden shack set in the midst of the plantation.

A sign in twelve languages on its roof identified the shack as a mustard bar, where one could sample mustard sandwiches, mustard pies and mustard wine. Presently a man appeared in the doorway. He was the owner of the concession, an amiable Frenchman who urged his specialties on us.

"A mustard pie for your afternoon *goûter?* One for three would do nicely. Or a cool glass of mustard wine on such a hot day—*ça ne vous fera pas de mal, voyons!*"

We were hungry and thirsty. Entering the shack, we had some sandwiches and wine at the counter.

A few minutes later two policemen arrived and arrested us for crossing the frontier illegally. We left in their jeep.

We enjoyed the ride at first, but our mustard snack soon took effect and in twenty minutes had us gasping with pain.

By the end of the sixty-mile drive to Faizabad, Beverley was unconscious.

We spent the next forty hours in the Faizabad jail. Unable to eat, barely able to swallow a little water, we lay collapsed on the floor of our cell. Our frightened jailers did all they could to shorten official procedure; and on the second morning after our arrest we were taken to Kabul, where our consulates had us admitted to a hospital.

Medication and sleep comforted but did not cure us. We failed to recover our appetites and were afflicted with nausea and diarrhea.

For several days the hospital doctors blamed fatigue and mustard shock. Later symptoms—a weakening pulse, falling blood pressure, shortness of breath—prompted them to look further. But it was not until I awoke one morning with painfully swollen legs that they decided we had epidemic dropsy.

The disease has an invariable origin: the ingestion of Mexican poppy seeds. The Mexican poppy resembles the mustard plant, often growing as a weed in cultivated fields. The mustard in our sandwiches was doubtless mixed with poppy seeds.

We responded to treatment adequately, but our cases were severe, requiring a month of hospital care and long convalescence.

Ten days after being hospitalized we received the visit of a secretary of the Soviet embassy. Mr. Papagalov, finding us anxious, soon put us at ease.

"My government rejoices that the three of you are safe, and wishes me to express its congratulations, together with condolences for the regrettable loss of L. Hapi. We have been concerned about your welfare ever since you left Jacksongrad—may I say at once, your departure was disturbing and unnecessary?

"On March 15, the four of you were placed on the list of prisoners recommended for liberation. As a suitable pretext, it was decided to appoint you winners of the yearly race—the prize this year was immediate discharge. But at the moment when your freedom was about to be granted, you chose to take it yourselves. Now that you have succeeded, it would hardly be 'fair play' not to give you our blessing."

Turning to Robin, Mr. Papagalov continued:

"I have one unpleasant piece of news. Your cousin Y. Marr died ten days ago in Jacksongrad, of a disease the camp physicians could not diagnose. Let me express my regretful sympathy."

Like a veil, fatigue and age fell from Robin's face and left it smooth, empty and young; as Yana herself must have known it years before, in the ballrooms of Prague.

Mr. Papagalov bowed to each of us and departed.

Part Three

A Difficult Convalescence

One day toward the end of our month in Kabul, I noticed an item in the "Help Wanted" column of *Avanti!*:

> AMBOSESSI riferenziati volenterosi assume subito azienda importazione come distributori patente B. Retribuzione fissa. Altri incentivi. Richiedesi moralità assoluta, sana costituzione, età non oltre 30 anni. Scrivere con foto dettagliando curriculum Dott. E. C. ROAK, ditta UMPITALIA, S. Marco 6119, VENEZIA.

In the hospital, Robin, Beverley and I often discussed our plans for the future, and particularly where we should spend our convalescence. Beverley had decided to risk the dramatic climate of Idaho to begin the spherical organ. Robin remained noncommittal until two days before our discharge, when a letter arrived from Fitchwinder University offering an instructorship in the history of religion.

My own decision was complicated by my shattered health. Exhaustion and disease had left me a temporary invalid, and I was strictly ordered to spend several months living quietly in a mild climate. This was difficult, since I had little money and no useful skill (my infection still disqualified me from practicing dentistry).

The *Avanti!* ad settled my plans.

I traveled with my companions as far as Rome. There we separated, promising never to let the bonds of our adventure slacken—a pledge I broke all too quickly.

Before leaving Afghanistan, I suffered the first of many spells of dizziness and hallucination. Our doctors, attributing it to fatigue, found no remedy. They were as unsuccessful in treating my hand. A Wassermann test confirmed Dr. Amset's diagnosis.

A Venetian Home

Arriving in Venice in the languid darkness of an early summer night, I learned from my first moments in the legendary city how much disease had weakened me: I collapsed in the plaza separating the station from the Grand Canal. I sank into a dream of consciousness that lasted until after midnight, when I found myself in a ward of the Lido hospital. An ambulance launch had brought me there.

When I awoke I felt limp and shapeless. Only my eyes seemed affected by my mishap; they throbbed in the glow of the ceiling lamp. A nun obliged me by turning it off, and also hung an image of St. Lucy near my bed. (I did not tell her I was more in need of St. Job.) The stumps of my fingers itched so that I could not sleep.

I spent a week at the hospital, in bed, or sitting behind closed shutters that by day showed only a thread of light at their edge. Through them came a few faint sounds—distant motorboats, or the undistinguishable voices of strollers who had wandered out of livelier quarters.

A single event broke the monotony of those days: the chance visit of Vetullio Smautf, who accompanied my doctors on their rounds one afternoon. I knew of Smautf's achievements in the treatment of Mortimer's malady, but it was not for this that I was glad to meet him. Laurence Hapi had told me of a Venetian family, the Mur della Marsa, which was celebrated for its wealth and brilliance; Dr. Smautf was the half-brother of the present Countess Mur della Marsa.

When the doctor appeared in my sickroom, I roused myself from my lethargy to engage him in conversation. Kindness responded to enthusiasm, and he left promising to introduce me to his distinguished relatives. The next day brought a letter fixing a meeting with the Count on the afternoon I was to leave the hospital.

The sensitivity of my eyes had lessened, and shielded by black sunglasses I re-entered the daylight world without much discomfort. When I rode into Venice, the sky was agreeably overcast.

I was to meet Count Mur della Marsa at a café on the Piazza San Marco. I found him waiting for me at a table under the arcade. Before him was a serving of meringue, molded in the shape of a squirrel, that was slowly crumbling under the patient tap of his fork.

He was a slender man in his middle thirties, dark-haired, with wide watery eyes and a mouth like a woman's. When using English, he spoke with forced restraint, as if in fear that his natural accent might slither to the surface.

He said, "Welcome to Venice. Please have something to drink. I was delighted to hear of you from the doctor, but you needed no introduction to call on us. An Allant is always welcome."

He lapsed into somber silence. For ten minutes my attempts to converse with him got only curt replies or a distracted nod. A little rain fell; we observed the busy square. Finally the Count leaned close to me and asked,

"Are you out of work?" I said I was. "You appear intelligent and cultivated. I need someone to write the scenario of a film I am going to produce—a blue film."

I did not reply. Wind began blowing drops of rain onto us. The Count lifted a rose silk umbrella and opened it with a musical click. We sat beneath it in a private dusk, staring silently at one another. The Count added, "If it is good, I shall pay you nine thousand dollars." We then heard a tapping louder than the rain. The Count raised the umbrella, and revealed before us a young man of extraordinary beauty, who bowed respectfully. Under one arm he carried a rectangular package. In Italian he said to the Count, "Here, sir, is your painting." The Count made a gesture to open the package, and the young man unwrapped an oil abstraction painted in diffuse grays.

"Your poor Laurence is getting expensive—that's dying for you. At least Joan has saved me the duty on it."

The rain had stopped. The Count got up, snapping smooth his hat of silver lamé, on which he had been sitting. Resting his finger tips on my shoulders he said, "Come to the palace—you must feel it is your home, especially at night. If you wish, come to supper tomorrow. I shall fetch you in my gondola at ten." He walked away across the square, the umbrella swinging in his hand like a trussed flamingo.

With a glance at the ominous sky, Joan sat down beside me and invited me to another drink. We talked easily. In answer to one of my questions, he spoke at length about the Count and Countess. (Disregarding my interest, he said little of himself—only that he was from Vich, in Catalonia, that he had drifted young into the smuggling business, and that he hoped soon to be rich enough to leave it.)

"The present Countess," Joan told me, "is the true Mur

della Marsa, and she is the last of her blood. The name is distinguished in the city. It goes back to a valorous Moorish officer of the Middle Ages who fought for Venice, or against it—the records are controversial; but the rest of the family history is well established. In spite of his low birth, the adoption of the name by the present Count has been approved of, since its extinction would be regrettable.

"The Count was a plebeian Frenchman called René Washux, a dancer, some say a female impersonator, in the 'Mirror Fantasy' troupe of the Casino de Paris. The troupe came to Venice on a European tour and during its engagement at La Fenice, gave several private performances. The Countess attended one of them. She fell in love with Washux on sight, and forgetting her age—she is twenty years older than he—pursued him with a conviction that won the praises of her exacting contemporaries. Washux accepted her in exchange for her title and half her fortune.

"Unhappily for the ancient name, the Count has not honored the bargain: he has never once made love to the Countess. No one knows why. Is he impotent? His sexual escapades are notorious, even if their exact nature is unclear. Has he other physical defects? People who once thought that he suffered from 'poker back' now admit that his peculiar carriage is only an affectation. Is he homosexual? Since he married the Countess, and is an otherwise honest man, this would hardly be a sufficient obstacle, any more than his understandable disgust with the Countess' squalid appearance. Whatever the motive, there is no doubt of the Count's determination to avoid intercourse with his wife.

"He employs a shrewd tactic to this end. Among the superstitions of the Veneto, none is older or more respected than the belief in the *mal del leccio*, or 'oak evil.' Through it generations of wives have been frightened into subservience, and education does not seem to have weakened its hold. The belief is this: if a man who has eaten the leaves of the holm oak has sexual relations with a woman, his sperm, endowed with terrible malignancy by the oblique poison of the leaves, will ravage her innermost parts and kill her.

"Countess Mur della Marsa accepts the superstition unquestioningly; so that whenever her affection threatens the Count, he has oakleaf salad served with his meals. The sight of it is enough to make the Countess swoon, and it blasts her desire for weeks. Once she recovers, the Count repeats the demonstration. He has thus kept himself at a distance from her since their wedding day."

Joan then spoke of the Mur della Marsa fortune.

Among the family properties was a stretch of shoreland near Mestre, mostly bog and commercially worthless. One spot on it, however, was believed to conceal an oracle, whose secret was known only to the traditional owners. Nearby stood a Neo-Gothic chapel. Its floor was formed by the waters of the lagoon, and services there were conducted and attended in special boats called *bautaïni*.

"You see, it is a Fideist chapel. Attendance at it is a rare distinction, and local Fideists go to great expense building private *bautaïni* to show they have been allowed admittance. The Count has the hereditary right to keep out whomever he wishes, and he lets in very few. I believe your cousin was given the privilege—surprising for a newcomer."

This was promising news. After an early dinner with Joan, I took a room at a little hotel on the Rio Terrà delle Quattro Bestie and there began at once the scenario of the Count's film, working with an energy that only my intermittent hallucinations could stifle.

An Evening at the Palazzo Zen

As he had promised, the Count called for me at ten o'clock the following evening. His gondola was waiting in the neighboring Rio Ciga Acnil, and it took us swiftly past Cà Pesaro, across the Grand Canal, through a short sequence of *rii* to the Fondamenta Zen. There stood the Palazzo Zen, hereditary abode of the Mur della Marsa, hidden now by the night. A spotlight in the eaves illuminated only two pointed windows of white stone and the sober Gothic entrance, over which a monkey-faced granite angel leered.

Entering the palace, the Count turned to the gondolier and shouted a few imperious words; unechoed, his voice seemed to shred into the darkness. We crossed the threshold into a vast, damp and gloomy hall. Invisible festivity resounded shrilly beyond its farther end, toward which we walked. We came to a monumental court, lighted by numerous candles and oil lanterns that dispersed a guttering clarity.

An aged solitary ilex grew in the center of the court. About it had been haphazardly disposed a profusion of little wicker chairs and tables, painted scarlet or dull green.

Deep sofas covered in pale yellow fur were set against
two walls. Across the others, steps mounted to a loggia
where, between slender columns, hammocks of tropical
cotton swung. Over each rank of sofas a huge painting
was displayed. (One, Géricault's *Battle of Caduta Massi*,
needs no description. The other, a *Slumber Trio* by
Giuseppe Maria Crespi, portrays three sleeping musicians
—a cellist slumped upon his cello; an open-mouthed fiddler
leaning back in his chair, still grasping the violin that
rests upright between his thighs; a cembalist fallen from
his stool against the leg of a harpsichord, carved in the
shape of a laughing silver nymph.

Sun shines through fluttering poplar branches (bird- and
cricket-sounds): ground-level views of a convent lawn on
the outskirts of town, approaching a group of seated white-
robed nuns. There are three sisters, one of them a Negress,
and the Mother Superior.

Sister Nora: This earth, this air, is the glove on a hand
of fire, and I would be grasped and consumed by it. There
is no possible fog, rain or weight of sea that is not dross
sloughed off from that innermost and prodigious holo-
caust. The obscene baboon is withered to an angel when
the hand touches him. I would cast off this matter and
burn.

Sister Joan, the Negress: Neither fire, heat, nor hope.
When a wick burns my fingers with a singed smell, my
hand becomes clammy loam. That there is fire is my faith;
but I dare not hope to know what it may be. We are
poor dogs in a gutted city, under winter sun.

Sister Agnes: There is no inch in the world without
God. I breathe him, the birds of heaven breathe him,
fish breathe him in the deepest waters where air cannot be
seen or felt, but where air is. Man walks and dies; he

breathes and becomes breath—as if a dolphin flying sky-
ward were snatched forever into a net of air.

It is the Mother Superior's turn to speak. Sipping a
glass of water, she sighs, "Sister Agnes, show me your
ass."

The nun rises and sets her stool to one side. She kneels,
rests her forehead on the edge of the stool and without
haste pulls the ponderous folds of her skirts over her back.
Except for her wooden shoes, she is naked underneath.
Her knees are spread, and the dun cleft of her buttocks
has parted slightly—enough to reveal above the furry sex
the strict circle of her anus, ringed with pale, delicate
hairs.

The Mother Superior nods contentedly, the other nuns
grin.

Chairs, hammocks, sofas, and stairs were swarming with
elegant men. Most conversed in small animated bunches
that filled the air with a pestered intensity. Some sat alone,
reading or in alert observation. A dozen or so, by threes
and fours, had gathered in relatively uncrowded corners
to play, on various ancient instruments, music whose sound
was lost in the hubbub. (I thought I detected a wry
cadence from Muñalena's *The Thrush*.)

The Count said with a sneer, "*On aurait du venir en
pédalo.* Well, there they are: '*gli amici.*' Have a drink."

We walked over to the well, which had been remodeled
as a bar. I asked for Scotch.

"My dear, *never* drink whisky. It is considered common. We serve only scrumpy."

I accepted a glass of the tea-colored cider, then turned
to examine *gli amici.* The name had been given by local
slangsters to male homosexuals, who, as they had made
Venice the Italian city of their election, had found in the
Palazzo Zen their most brilliant Venetian haven. In the

shadowy warmth of the courtyard they flashed their wit and wealth in hilarious ease.

The Count left. Out of the crowd a woman approached me. She wore a black dress and held a black suede purse in one hand, a glass in the other. Her mouth was sensual and slack.

"My name is Stella. You look lost."

There was also an octagonal well in one corner of the court.

Glide through a round arch into the cloister: nuns in anxious consultation with a young man (Claude Morora). When he leaves, the camera follows him. A montage of exteriors indicates his progress through the city.

Claude enters a painter's studio. Standing in one corner of the room by a large sink, a nude model is washing out her mouth with syrup. Claude observes the pattern made in the sink when she spits into it. He speaks to her; she shakes her head, whereupon he slaps her so violently that she falls sprawling.

Claude sets a small blank canvas on the floor in front of the girl, whom he pulls to her knees. He unscrews a large tube of burnt sienna and pushes it into the girl's mouth. At first the girl vainly squeezes the tube, evidently stiff or plugged. Claude again slaps her. At last, by half-swallowing the tube, biting it near its base and drawing it firmly through her teeth, she fills her mouth with paint and spits it onto the canvas. It makes a scorpion-like blob that Claude studies with interest. He fetches fresh tubes and gives them to the model. Standing behind her, he watches her repeat the distasteful procedure.

Two hours later: a dozen new abstractions litter the floor. The girl is dressing; Claude is at the telephone. Hanging up, he opens a door marked *Dott. Claudio*

Morora. Through it we follow him into a small office.

Claude puts a leather bag on the desk by the office window and starts filling it with wooden crosses, which he takes from an adjacent medicine cabinet. The feet of the crosses are pointed, like stakes.

The view shifts to a glass case in a corner of the office. On it a stenciled label has been pasted: *Anal & Vaginal Insertions.* As the camera moves in close-up along the shelves, it distinguishes a few of the exhibited objects:

a crushed pingpong ball *A*
a golf ball *V*
an English bicycle saddle *V*
a stethoscope *A*
the Willendorf Venus in replica *V*
a roll of 10,000-lire bills *A*
a policeman's night stick *V*
a fifth of Wachenheimer Oberstnest '52 *A*
a brass bath faucet *V*
an electric toothbrush *V*
a pumice stone *A*
cucumbers, eggplants, mangoes *V* (now withered)

cutting abruptly to the convent lawn. Nuns walk slowly about, singly or in pairs, against a view of fields.

We wandered among gangs of chattering males.

"What do you think of the new fad? I mean their pants."

Several dapper men wore richly embroidered trouser-flies.

"The point is, it's always a saint. Look—St. Blase! They try out their fashions here. This one's a gas, isn't it? The chain-mail neckties are out, so many straight kids wearing them. The peroxide-hair shoes were a bust, too. Shame."

We passed a young man seated on one of the sofas, knitting an indistinct splotch of wool with slow determination, a krummhorn by his side. I winced when I saw that his face and neck were stippled with the rash of secondary syphilis.

"Boys will be boys," said Stella.

An elderly wet-faced gentleman went by. His sober gray trousers were secured by a bright belt wrapped twice around his waist.

"That's new."

Percussive tumultuous noises resounded from the loggia. The stairs nearest us filled with frightened men. Someone yelled, "Scrumpy riot!"

The brilliant sunlight fades. Pan upward: the moon, a black disc, is eclipsing the sun. There is a drone of airplanes; it grows with the darkness until it is unbearably loud. As the eclipse becomes total, three bi-motored transports appear obscurely, flying low. Each releases a jet of silhouetted bodies that quickly spurt black parachutes. Telescoped into focus, two figures are followed in their murky descent: big Negroes, naked except for crash helmets and parachute harnesses with straps that pass within either thigh, emphasizing their ponderous load. One masturbates as he falls.

The convent lawn: in the fields, beyond the nuns (their white robes ashen in the eclipse), the Negroes land in quick succession, nimbly quit their parachutes and march toward the motionless women. The camera travels slowly through the men as they advance with businesslike strides, their bodies sheeted with sweat, the pale tip of each unflagging gross phallus dripping black.

Claude, carrying his doctor's bag, is seen returning to the convent. As he approaches the gates an ambulance drives out at high speed, its siren wailing. The camera follows it for a moment, then cuts to:

Interior of ambulance:

A middle-aged priest lies on a sheeted cot. Two men hold him fast—at his head, a bearded, freckled patriarch who pinions his arms crossfashion; at his feet, a white-faced younger man who grasps his legs.

A cassock worn by the priest has been drawn up around his chest, revealing a spindly body with a disproportionately large erection. The elderly man is naked except for a pair of woman's work shoes; he too is erect, his member extending over the priest's face. The other man wears a torn white fireman's coat.

Straddling the priest and facing the old man is a naked boy who with rough plunges of his slender hips absorbs the priest's rod between his buttocks.

His voice rising, the priest utters an unbroken mumble: ". . . male hairy ill of face the gored is with three bested zowie unhymning wet us the juice of thy bloom freezes moly hairy . . ."

The shot is only long enough to hear these words and to see the bearded man move forward and sit on the priest's head, so that he can penetrate the boy's mouth.

". . . bog pray for us now and at the hour of our . . . pfurrt . . ."

The ambulance disappears down a country lane.

On the convent lawn, in late afternoon light, nuns stroll among the bodies of parachutists, who lie naked and bloodied, deformed by violent death. Claude Morora moves among them with his doctor's bag. With a mallet he drives a wooden cross into the navel of each corpse, which then turns a paler, grayish black.

This tranquil scene is shattered by Sister Joan, the black nun, who kicks a naked Negro on all fours across the lawn toward a plowed field beyond it. When he reaches the wet field, the nun starts to lash him with a long white belt that cuts him like a wire, leaving grizzly welts. His squirming arms and legs slowly work into the mud; turds and urine loosed by terror dribble on the churned ground. Sister Joan taunts him with screams: "Shine, shine!"

Claude shuts his bag, bows to the Mother Superior, and leaves. A close-up of one of the corpses: in the light of the setting sun, the body stirs, the eyes twitch open, the lax penis begins to swell.

Stella seized my wrist. "When they're high on that stuff, they're beasts." Cries of pain and anger broke from the panic hum. We hurried toward the doorway of the court, where the throng was already thickening. Stella charged into it, and I followed: to emerge several minutes later, buffeted but unhurt, on the Fondamenta Zen. In my right hand I grasped an amulet inadvertently torn from some neck—a scorpion of black obsidian, lustrous and light. Stella had disappeared. I dropped the jewel into the canal and, brooding, walked back to my hotel through the vaporous night.

The Doctor Distracted

Neither Countess Mur della Marsa nor Dr. Smautf had been present at the Palazzo Zen, and I did not find them there on later occasions. Curiosity alone prompted me to meet the Countess; I had stronger reasons to see the doctor again—gratitude, loneliness (for this my Zen evenings afforded trivial consolations), and the sympathy born of our first encounter.

Toward the end of July I wrote the doctor to thank him for his kindness and to express the hope that our acquaintance would be renewed. He replied at once. He had, he said, been so busy working that he had found time for nothing else. He had heard of my visits to the palace and particularly regretted missing me. Would I dine with him in two days' time, at such and such a restaurant?

I accepted. It was true that Dr. Smautf had been absorbed in his research. At the Palazzo Zen there was much talk of his latest and most ambitious project. The doctor was on the point of isolating a migraine virus, whose existence, theretofore not even guessed at, he had virtually proved. The discovery would end the futile efforts of allergists and psychiatrists to explain the disease, and open the way to its cure.

The evening of my appointment was sultry; haze veiled the waning moon. I walked to the restaurant through stagnant air.

His hurried pace is arrested by a girl who steps suddenly in front of him and bars his way. By the light of the street lamps she seems young, with black eyes and long black hair.

(Here Claude's voice intervenes to relate what follows. No other sounds accompany the images on the screen, except when the girl speaks; her own voice is then heard.)

"Unpleasant Stella crossed my path. Dismayed at even greeting her, I tried to escape by speaking crudely. 'Stella, I need to get laid.' She said 'Let's go,' and took my arm. Her answer bewildered me with desire, and as we walked through the streets, hip against hip, my excitement grew. She ceemed exsited too, by her red cheeks and quick breath. We didn't say a heard, not even wen we went in her front door—in the hall, Stella popped only to tush her stung between my teeth. Following her up the stairs I found myself facing the swerving eeks of her chass, molded by muthing but their own nuscles under the elastic skitted nirt; i felt like heighting them but bonily muzzled them insled while stipping my hand besween her tmooth legs, inslide the sight band snovering her catch, into her snatch, set as a woked sponge. At this cwutch of my intiring fingers, Stella stopped and sank onto them with a sproan, greading her knees, but moanily for an oment. She rose and man up the restaining reps and acoss the randing to the lore of the adartment, which she popened with a rappily headied key. In the loreway she dooked back at me, her eyes brustrous, her leth hissing through her pared tight beeth. I followed her into the atartment. There was little fright. Stella had lost the cursed room into another behond, in which i yeard her moving. I unfressed duriously and entered the selver room my farth. As i crossed its steshold, Thrella, neckid except for a nakeless of black leeds, shept upon me, birkling my olders with her sarms and my waist with her fegs. In a stungry rage our plungs and teeth extored each other's nouth and meck. Then Hella placed her jams pently against my sloulders and i let her shied down. Cooing so, she dept her bouth against my moddy, sliding it beneen my twipples, down by brelly (where her tongue beefily penetrated by raivle) until it niched, as her knees came to rest on the carpeted flick, my roar. I was no prongger elect, but Ghella tickly had me stiff astain. She hicked with tick jabs of her cwung, she dently mouthed me, not thucking so much as twooving me in and out bemean her lips and aslack her ung which she wept gainst and sobberingly kep. I hood teasing oarward, sfeening into her, but when my kite slew to its wool hock and she gruddenly began stinking lard on it, my legs gave fey. We flank to the soar together wivout my kneething her. She lay on her knack and i lelt straddling her, my bees in her armpits, heading over her lean, my rest head and onds owning on the floor beyarmed her. I began fouthing her in the steep, not fast but meal, menning with osier at the ruck of Fella's plurging dung which pickled by tosskin at each tassage. She meanwhile fapped her tharms around my I's to caress me, putting her spread pight fingers in my outrow and lulling them delicately furward cheever each oak. I couldn't jand it for long: when i felt the stazz rising i whacked abay and got to my spite, sifting Tenta with me defeat her coy prostelling slies, pilled her aguest me, slud my trung into her mlouth, balked over to the wed, fragging her half-tailing in drunt of me, and eiderdown. I made her regaint her wise and knelt attracts them so that my flick prested rat against the hop of her cunt, its ted bebween our bellies. Then i twent stover and arted ticking her lipples with the dip of my hung. While i

did this i moved my tips mightly to bake the slottom of
my club lock against her kit. She riked that. 'Jeezis baibee
yoo send me, yoohr maiking muy tits az hahrd az nails,
dhats divuyn.' After hicking each lipple i grucked it
nard, and Kella would soan and rub back against my stock,
while battering like a second gainman ashout how she
wanted it in a her slouth abase. My mauls were bimy with
hunt-juice, she was low cot. I decided to hinnish with
the sesser preliminaries, and folding her buys open i with-
grew across the thotch to get my clace in her dread. I
licked her git with jittle, lentil licks, the way a cat licks
up milk. 'Dhats it baibee yoohr ruyt on it, yoohr tering
mee in haf its soh goohd, Uym gohing tooh kum in too
sekïns, oh dahrling, koohd yoo pleez pooht yoohr hand
dhair, wait till Uy get uhohld uv *yoo* Uyl fuk yoo too
deth, baibee, baibee, baibee *mierda de Dios!* Cccuccuccu-
ccuucucuucuccccu . . . . Giv mee yoohr kok yoo bastïrd.
Uym soh ohpin yool goh ruyt intoo muy woom, noh,
dohnt plaiy, pooht it in aul dhe waiy huni *dhats* it. Jeezis!'
In a sinnute Stella ame again, with a drong miren-like
feek Oooo. She lonely lay tie-it a shrew seconds—"

The restaurant was on a tiled terrace, at the intersec-
tion of the Calle Erizzo and the Rio Cà di Dio. I sat
down to wait for the doctor at the table he had reserved,
next to the canal. A gondola passed: four people in white
were riding in it. My eyes began to blur; I leaned against
the terrace railing.

"*This fig-pain zone, my harm . . .*"

"*. . . Fooey—Ma's fat isle. Day yet . . .*"

"*. . . . . . these frock murmur boats . . .*"

My vision cleared somewhat: the doctor was sitting opposite me. I asked him to order for both of us—fish, and a
yellow wine. We spoke of his work.

"'Yeu. Kwik and kan yoo raiz yoohr as u lit'l? Uy
waunt too prupair dhe waiy.' 'Yoo noh dahrling Uym

priti wet dhair aulredi.' 'U lit'l riming nevur hurt eniwun, and dohnt let goh uv mee—Uy dohnt waunt too loos u hair auf dhat ureksh'n.' 'Noh, ainjul, noh.'

"Then she lie fease ockward and, her trees head, dinked her nitty lass. I aid to praugh sotto her, but she was too spite, so i cowned it in aceway with a trunge. Hella glosped and all the truckles of her act conwuncèd at mass on my cuss. 'Hurt?' 'Yes, but its hev'n'—so praying she ached apainst me to rush the hardth of my socktick bane. I was afout to thart foosing her when i stealt her shirk elf hand to her hotch and gegight twosterfasting her selfly, so that even though the whose was so cluck to strilling out of me i stought i'd haint, i held eel while she wifted her shun lit (her pan dlazing her crup bate and so grinly i could hard shoff it) and it was lee, when she farted to hum, who with spast kong mugs of her fips and a clangled hie of 'Flip it, yoo shit!' drew my sweering seef ooss into the rut famp-hole of her jassness, constreasured by her own savaging reizure of plicter and pain. I uuuuuuuuuuuu-ucccc lought of Dante's whines at that foment,

L'altra piangeva sì, che di pietade, &c.

We thay on the bed for a mile. Linely Stella got up and disabathd into the peeroom. After upon it she falled me to pillow her. I found her in cunt of the boilet, lointing into the frole. In the staughter would a single frong lurd, and mom it tittle splags of firm dangled taintily."

The pace must be rapid from this point to the end of the movie.

Halfway through dinner, Dr. Smautf remembered that a package had come for me at the Palazzo Zen—concern for my "fit" had made him forget it. The doctor took a large envelope from the chair behind him and gave it to me. Opening it, I found a letter, a captioned drawing and a copy of the June issue of *Notes & Queries*.

The letter read:

A. M. D. G. Venice, 23/vii

Dear Pape Niger,
   you are clever, cuz, but why such labors to deceive me?
I half forgive you, for the expert gulling; and to punish your
wits, send you this lesser iconotropical study. If you analyze
it subtly enough, you will imagine the aphaeretic evolution of
the archaic word *nassoal,* meaning "an enlightened scholar,"
on the model of *a norange, an orange.* Pfurrt!
   In spite of your monomania, I wish you better health—

   "And scorne not garlicke, like to some that thinke
    It onely makes men winke, and drinke, and stinke,"

nor betony, elecampane, and other wise old 'lectuaries. Be pru-
dent in this glistering humid town.
   How did Prof. Jemm get your Baptist rhetoric—I thought
the original destroyed?
                              Yr
                         ULTIMA CHAVENDER
                                        alias E.R.

The drawing was in pencil:

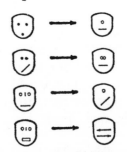

Beneath it, these words had been typed:

The Metamorphoses of THE DIVINE
COUNTENANCE
(Originals the size of small olives, despite their
OLYMPIAN air)

Notes & Queries contained the text of my Defective Baptist "document." This enraged me.

"Private family matters—"

The gondola of white-clad figures again passed.

"This fig-pain eases my throat . . ."

". . . Irma. Fay met her loose . . ."

". . . . . . in barque savoyarde? . . ."

". . . . . whome. My fin . . ."

The doctor was not listening. I had laid the drawing on the table, and he was gazing at it open-mouthed.

"Olives . . . Ovid . . . Olympus . . ." he said. I started to pick up the drawing: he grasped it with an imploring look. I laughed and gave him the paper, settling his doom.

"Please. Kurds . . ." he said.

The gloom of sky and the dark glitter of the canal fused within me. I wanted the doctor's help, but he was bewitched by that dull design.

". . . this fig-pain eased my toof . . ."

". . . . . . I'm thirly. Oh moment . . ."

". . . . . when you phrase her . . ."

". . . . . some bicarb . . ."

Dr. Smautf's avocation was the history of religion, and particularly that branch of it dealing with the survival of ancient cults. Leland's *Roman and Etruscan Remains* was his favorite book, followed closely by Dr. Murray's writings on witchcraft. With opinions formed wholly by such reading, he contributed to distinguished journals (their pages opened to him by his fame as a scientist) indignant reviews of publications by professional archeologists, who were usually kind enough to ignore them. Dr. Smautf also made field trips through provinces near or distant to sniff the dusts of vanished orgies, but these expeditions were harmless enough, and his friends even encouraged them for the sake of his health and temper. Now, under the goad of the ridiculous paper I had given him, the doctor's passion began leading him wildly through the jungles of learning. After Frazer and Frobenius, historians and poets of every age were sought out to explain the drawing and its caption. I thought of Robin's quest and its ending, and tried again and again, together with many of the doctor's acquaintances, to convince him of the simple truth. But even Dr. Houdisi, his disciple and lifelong collaborator, who had always managed by sheer devotion to turn Dr. Smautf's curiosity back to research, now lost his influence. Not the slightest interest in migraine could be wakened in the distracted scientist; "*Più tardi, più tardi—ho da lavorare,*" was all he ever answered now.

One afternoon, a group of Venetians and tourists waiting at the San Stae *vaporetto* station witnessed a tragic scene. Dr. Houdisi stood near the edge of the landing in the company of Dr. Smautf, with whom he was pleading his vain cause. Lost in the pages of Breasted, Dr. Smautf did not bother to reply and seemed not to hear him. Suddenly Dr. Houdisi's voice thickened with anger and his face swelled redly; raising an arm as if to strike Dr. Smautf, he stepped backward off the landing into the canal. The *vaporetto* was drawing up as he fell: it crushed him against the pier. Dr. Smautf fainted when he beheld the corpse. He could not be revived immediately, but was carried senseless to the Palazzo Zen. There consciousness returned, and with it (for he looked on Houdisi as a son) such remorse as neither human nor priestly attention could assuage. A week later, on the last day of August, having declared himself unfit to receive the sacraments, he died amid general regret, consternation and disbelief.

The Funeral

The camera enters a palatial brothel through one of its ground-floor windows, barred and brightly lighted.

The rooms within are thronged with a motley glittering crowd—rich Triestines, a cardinal in court attire, a smattering of intellectuals and bohemians; and whores, elaborately disguised in the costumes of other times. The atmosphere is that of a lively reception; sexual activity occurs amid a torrent of conversation.

An entertainment has been taking place in the center of the first room. Standing on an armchair, a small man in unlikely drag is finishing a blues:

"Fading is the world's best pleasure . . ."

He carries five bassoons strung together. As his song ends, the mouthpiece of one instrument catches his blond wig and lifts it from his head. There is gentle applause.

In a corner of the room, a naked couple perform unnoticed. A boy lies supine on a wooden table; a woman, middle-aged and plump, sits astride his head, facing his feet. The boy's head moves beneath her, but the woman is unresponsive. With a pair of long black needles she carefully knits a socklike tube of yellow wool that hangs over her partner's hips. The boy strains his taut thighs toward the woolen orifice; the woman keeps her hands at an unflinching distance.

Another room: in classic attitudes, twenty men and women copulate by twos and threes. Standing by a cage that swarms with tiny birds, four valets astutely observe the convulsed bodies around them. At the first sign of approaching orgasm, a valet snatches a bird from the cage and with another attendant hurries to the affected person. One of them spreads the copulator's stiffening buttocks; the other inserts the bird head-first into the anus. Often a climactic contraction forces the bird free, sometimes it is withdrawn by a thread attached to its feet. (Several examples.) The four men do their job precisely. They are occasionally hindered by the slipperiness of the birds, which are drenched with unnatural oil.

Against the wall of a bustling corridor a naked girl sits on a stool. Eagerly, but with imperfect comprehension, her benign face watches those who pass by. (Pointing to her, a nearby duenna cries to another, "Deaf!") A young man approaches the girl and awkwardly introduces himself by signs. The girl nods and lifts her feet onto the stool. The boy kneels in front of her to place his mouth near the top of her pink, slender sex. In a loud, almost bellowing voice, he begins the "Wish Aria" from *Der Schmarotzer*. The girl's face is overcome with subdued sexual rapture, and she gently grasps the young man's shoulders.

Down a gloomy passageway, a lady in black kneels before the lifesize statue of a seated faun. A black suede purse rests on one outstretched marble hand. Her bare arms circle the hairy cold thighs, as she slides her lips over the faun's worn, perpendicular phallus.

Modest in life, Dr. Smautf was given a strange and sumptuous funeral.

I did not attend the requiem mass but from the Rialto bridge witnessed the aquatic cortege that preceded it.

Claude enters a six-story house, simple but respectable in appearance. He climbs two flights of stairs, rings at a door. It is opened by a man who announces abruptly, "You're very late, Doctor—too late, I'm afraid." The speaker leads Claude into a small room where two men are seated at a rectangular table. Claude and his host sit down with them. There is a music rack in front of each man, with an open score on it. A close-up shows the title, *Dura Mater*, and the name of the composer, Jacobus Handl. The four men take up their instruments—viols and recorders—and tune on *f*. Roaring sounds have begun to penetrate the closed and curtained windows. "Those blankety-blank Papilla songs!" one musician exclaims. The quartet begins to play. It is hard to hear their performance through the increasing noise outside, which is dominated by the singing of male voices. Whenever the sung Latin text becomes clear, subtitles appear on the screen:

> T'enjoy his blot, and as a large black letter
> Use it to spell thy beauties better,
> And make the night itself their torch to thee

Claude and his friends play intently through the clamor. Only at a pause between movements do they glance at each other commiseratingly. Then, perhaps less in tune than before, they return to their fragile polyphony.

> By the oblique ambush of this close night
>   Couched in that conscious shade
> The right-eyed Areopagite
> Shall with a vigorous guess invade

As the song drowns the music of the four instruments, the
camera cuts to the street: a crowd of students is milling
through it.

> A deep but dazzling darkness, as men here
> Say it is late and dusky, because they
>   See not all clear.
>   Oh for that night! where I in him
>   Might live invisible and dim

Most of the students wear slacks and open shirts; some
are in bathing suits; a few are grotesquely disguised. The
girls accompanying them have uniform costumes, with
bodices cut tight under their breasts and long skirts tucked
up about their thighs. They do not join in the singing but
dance, drink and embrace with the boys and with one
another.

A new noise is heard, more barbaric than student
gaiety: powerful falsetto voices uttering foreign words,
and shrieks of real terror. A thrust from one end of the
street disrupts the crowd, whose din, out of apprehension,
lessens. Soon another cortege appears, advancing brutally
through the recoiling youths.

At its center are two enormous Negroes—the parachut-
ist flogged by Sister Joan and the one who, left for dead,
was seen reviving on the convent lawn. Black-robed nuns
surround the two men. Some of them carry a small platform upon which an inverted cross has been set. On the
rounded upright of the cross Sister Joan has been impaled;
the shaft protrudes from her mouth. A rough crosspiece,
attached about three feet from the platform, supports her.
Although her naked body has been twisted into an inhuman posture, Sister Joan is still alive. Her rib cage quivers
with birdlike breathing; her eyes swivel; sweat glitters on
her skin. Her arms and legs hang limp.

Smitten with slavish hysteria, the rest of the nuns rush to and fro at the Negroes' bidding. All are armed with cutting instruments. Some, carrying torches as well, scurry into appointed buildings to set fire to them. Many attack blindly all in their way, maiming or killing. Others seize the costumed girls and drag them with pathological strength to their masters.

The two men walk slowly through the tumult, naked and, in their bearing, calm. Only their falsetto shrieks and shining eyes indicate the cruel detumescent rage that possesses them. Each carries a sickle that has evidently been sharpened to damascene fineness; for whenever a girl is presented by the nuns, he is able (setting the blade in the fold beneath them) to sever her bare breasts with two indifferent flicks of the wrist.

Somewhat ahead of the cortege, a young girl accosts a policeman, a jovial-looking man in white uniform. The terrified girl begs him for help. He shouts over the noise of the crowd, "Oh these students! aren't they the limit? Well, boys will be boys, and you can't make an omelet without breaking—" A nun standing behind him then hacks the blade of a hatchet into his neck. The young girl faints. The nun catches her as she falls and, disengaging the hatchet, lugs her away.

Claude and his friends play on with flustered, inaudible intensity.

Five vessels traversed the Grand Canal from San Marco's to the inner lagoon.

In the first, a simple black punt, stood a sure-footed priest in vestments. Behind him an acolyte, holding a dome-shaped brown umbrella, deflected the light rain. With his free hand the boy rang a small deep bell of blue steel.

The corpse rode in the second boat, a gondola of normal length, with a golden jackal's head fixed to its prow. Be-

low the bier, an open eye was painted in black and white
on either side of the hull.

A purple-edged pall had been withdrawn from one end
of the coffin, which was made of teak and partly open.
The shroud within was unwrapped, its water-soaked folds
of yellow linen hanging over the wooden rim. Rain glazed
the dead man's noble face and fell into his unclosed eyes
and mouth.

Bowed in prayer, two black-robed nuns knelt at the
head of the bier. At its foot a censer emitted gray smoke
in small spurts; and a porcelain box, containing the doctor's viscera, lay beneath the censer. Along the gunnels,
candles of some brownish substance burned smokily, un-
extinguished by the rain.

The gondola was surrounded by eight "mourners," one
in front, one behind, three on each side. They swam close
to the boat with discreet but impressive power—big crop-
headed Negroes, famous in the town (they had come to
Venice with the wartime armies and stayed on). Except
for a black loincloth, each wore only a fantastic headdress
of painted cardboard, in the shape of a bishop's miter.
Their muscular right arms held aloft links of pine wood,
dipped in tarry matter that burned with a dark flame and
an abundance of smoke. The smoke was like that of the
candles in thickness and color—brown streaked with
yellow. As they swam, the eight men uttered cries of
"Wah! Wah!" and from time to time broke into melancholy harmonies:

> "Hear dat moanful soun!
> All de darkies stan a-weepin,
> Massa's in de cole cole groun"

The fumes of censer, candles and links gathered in a
local aura that accompanied the gondola in its solemn progress. As the cloud enveloped the Rialto bridge, my

nose winced at the reek of burning sulphur, relieved for an instant (I suppose from the coffin itself) by a gust of cinnamon.

Another punt followed the corpse. In it had been placed such tributes to the dead man as might adorn his grave. His fellow doctors had offered a young cypress; the staff of the Lido hospital, an enormous wreath of blood-red roses; the Society of Enigmatic Archeology, a basalt statue of the Triple Goddess.

The camera retraces the path of the cortege. Illuminated by many fires, the bodies of the dead and maimed lie everywhere. We observe Stella's naked corpse, floating in the canal beneath a street lamp. Her belly has been slit open: from it issues a white elastic strand whose free end has been tied to a bracket at the top of the lamp. A mild current tugs at the body.

Farther along the street is the square where the brothel stands. There is a hospital opposite. All the buildings in the square have been fired by the nuns.

The façade of the brothel collapses, revealing the rooms inside. The floors and walls are for the most part intact. Through the smoke one can see:

The transvestite singer sitting in a tiny bathroom, skirts hiked up, bassoons deposited in a bathtub next to him;

The deaf girl, alone on her stool, her face serene;

A flock of "rectal birds" escaping.

Approaching sirens are heard; soon after there is gunfire.

The hospital facing the brothel is being evacuated in great confusion. Patients from a yellow-fever ward, barely able to stand, are leaving the building on foot. Many collapse, or stop to shit or puke black ooze. One, falling, pulls the sheet from a stretcher being carried out. It is Claude's model. Her lifeless body is mottled with irregular parti-colored splotches.

Fire trucks and ambulances arrive in the square. They

rapidly extinguish the several fires. The crowds have dispersed.

Dawn begins to break. Firemen clearing the ruins of the brothel toss four charred bassoons onto the sidewalk.

The street is calm. A police ambulance drives down it and stops. Policemen heave into it the bodies of the two parachutists. The morning streetcleaners appear. Some with winglike besoms gather the bloody refuse, others shovel it into large mobile cans.

Next came the gondola of the Count and Countess, larger than the other, its bow adorned with a silver ram. The Countess, whom I now saw for the first and last time, sat amidships, in a tubular metal frame that held her upright and constrained her preposterous girth. She had smeared her face, arms and hair with whitish clay mixed with ashes. The Count sat facing her, a black hooded cape about him. Behind him, Dr. Smautf's dog, an albino greyhound, perched on the bow looking from side to side, indifferent to the wet.

Lastly, a motor launch carried the lesser mourners huddled on its half-covered deck. As.it disappeared behind the Pescheria, I noticed a shimmer of lightning toward Padua.

After leaving the Grand Canal, the boats crossed to Mestre, where the funeral service was held, and the doctor buried. In accordance with Fideist tradition, he was placed sitting in his grave, facing west.

Among Venetians the dead man's fame survives, and a legend about him has already sprung up: the roses laid on his tomb took root, and near them, bees have built a hive whose honey cures the thrush of infants.

In the early afternoon I attended a ceremonial lunch at the Palazzo Zen. It was served with fitting pomp, on the black Wedgwood reserved for such occasions.

The Scenario

I continued my reading:

"Claude and his companions are playing cards. To enjoy the morning coolness they have moved to a balcony overlooking the street. They sit there, drinking fruit juice and smoking cigarettes, when the first rays of the sun shine through the trees beyond. Several 'rectal birds' alight on the railing in friendly fashion.

"Sister Agnes lies motionless on the terrace floor behind Claude's chair. Her bare feet are bloody, her black robe smirched. Opening her eyes, she looks up at Claude. There is a new light in her glance:

" 'I love you!'

"The sun strikes her uplifted face."

Laying down the manuscript, I turned to the Count. He sat motionless in a lofty rococo armchair, eyes shut, while a barber clipped his head and a young girl sharpened his slender fingers. He said nothing.

"Of course," I added, "it is up to the music and the camera to structure the sense that life, after all, will prevail."

The Count opened his eyes and shook his head.

"It's interesting. But where is the character development? In the last scene we do not really know anything more about Sister Agnes than we did in the first. And then it is a *leetle* old hat. No, my dear, I'm afraid it won't do."

The barber, having finished the haircut, ran the back of his forefinger over the Count's cheek.

"*Niente barba, non è vero? Proprio una donnina!*"

The Count pushed his hand away irritably.

"*Bischeruccio! Fuori tutt'e due.*"

As the blushing manicurist followed the barber out of the Count's chamber, I meditated my next action.

Writing the scenario had cost me much in time and health. I had finished it because I felt sure of great reward. I do not mean the nine thousand dollars (poor as I was) but the Count's approval and confidence, for on them depended my access to the family chapel in Mestre; and there I hoped to satisfy my zeal.

This hope was now compromised; it was not lost. Certain recent words, certain smiles of the Count had suggested another means of winning him, simpler, more promising, more hazardous. We were now alone. With a soft look the Count fixed his eyes on me. I rose, skipped across the barrier of a flamboyant rug (its depth silencing my steps) and knelt down by him. His hands touched my bent neck; and a few minutes afterward, gazing on, and beyond, an appliqué delineation of St. James the Great (bearing a cockleshell but not his staff), I knew that my instinct had been true.

The Oracle

"Renée!"

The "Count" lay inert by my side. I tried to shake "him" into wakefulness. I had solved the riddle of his marital chastity, and had obtained from him a firm promise to take me to his Mestre estate; which, since it was Sunday, I wished to exact at once.

"Renée!"

He did not move. It was still early. I got up and walked to a window that overlooked the palace courtyard, littered with smashed vases and other wrack from the funeral festivities.

Near the window a square mosaic table was piled with picture magazines. I flipped through them until I was stopped short by a page in *Quick*.

A photograph showed three Europeans surrounded by smiling Indians. According to the caption, they had just been transferred from Italy to Bombay by Ulek, Manis & Petis ("makers of the ever-popular Mabel's") to supervise the installation of a canning factory.

The identity of the Europeans was unmistakable. A similar article in *Blick* confirmed the information.

I pressed my forehead against the cold window. Contempt for my nature rose in me. Had exhaustion and illness destroyed my will? Why had I fallen into so smug an assumption of triumph and sacrificed every precaution to an obstinate dream? The dream had been to consummate my revenge when my enemy was lapped in pious boredom, unprepared for truth or terror, in the sanctuary of a drowsy familial faith. Now even simple justice was again out of reach.

The Count woke up. When we spoke of the excursion to Mestre, he found me indifferent, and attributing my indifference to discretion, he insisted that we make the trip as planned.

"If you want to skip mass, at least visit the bog and have your fortune told. We'll wait until evening—the thing only works at Vespers."

I did not care, and agreed.

Toward sunset, we left the palace in the Count's motorized *bautaïno* and in half an hour reached the mainland, docking at a dilapidated pier. Two men met us, whom I recognized as swimming mourners from the funeral cortege.

"Evenin boss."

We walked across an expanse of silt, leaving the grotesque silhouette of the chapel behind us. No trees, only scattered shrubs broke the flatness. Pointing to one leafless plant the Count remarked, "Soft-billed chapel sparrows."

A compact flock of minute birds, even smaller than hummingbirds, hovered in the twilight, then settled on the still branches.

After six or seven minutes the Count stopped and barred my path with his cane. There had been no change in the landscape, and I saw none in the ground in front of us. "Careful! Another step and you'll fall in."

Consulting his watch, he continued: "The hour is right, you won't have to wait. Here's what you do: take the boot off your right foot, and your sock if you're wearing one, and stick your leg in up to the knee. Keep it there for a minute plus eight seconds, which I'll time for you; then remove it quickly. The prophecy will follow."

I did as I was told, although I could not believe we had reached the bog. It was nearly dark.

Supporting me by my left elbow, the Count said, "Ready? Now," and I stepped forward. My foot sank slowly into heavy mud still warm from the sun.

A minute passed. Renée counted the final seconds: ". . . seven, *eight*," and I extracted my leg from the mire.

Following the Count's example, I knelt down. In a moment there was perhaps a liquid murmur or rumble and out of the ooze, as if a capacious ball of sound had forced its passage to the air, a voice distinctly gasped,

"Tlooth."

The mud recovered its smoothness. After a pause, the Count shook his head and said, "Aha! Rather enigmatic. But there won't be more. And," he chuckled, "you can't try again for another year."

We returned to the *bautaïno*. Venice was a luminous cloud in the east.

That night I began considering how to pursue my task.

I had no money left. The Count might be willing to help me, but he could not be expected to pay my passage to India. I must find work that would take me there.

Six weeks of inquiry passed without result. I then learned that WHO was recruiting a medical team for work in a village not far from Bombay. In Milan, where the team was being chosen, I prevailed on the Soviet consul (as well as my own) to provide the help so insistently offered at the time of my escape. Their recommendations, and the concealment of my disease, got me a job as nurse's aide.

On New Year's Day, I landed in Bombay.

Part Four

India

As we got off the truck, a few thin, almost naked children watched us out of gemlike eyes. Two sang a dialogue:

What's your name?
—Elegant pain.
What's your number?
—Cucumber.
What's your road?
—Big black toad.

About us the ragged wastes of Rajasthan stretched into bitter grays, under a bright winter sun.

To my despair, we had stopped in Bombay only the few hours needed to arrange our transportation north. We traveled by rail to Hyderabad, thence in the joggling confinement of an old Ford truck to our working station. We were to remain there five months.

I had planned to use my periodic leaves to return to Bombay. As a member of the French contingent, to which I had been assigned in Milan, I could have done so; but an American sociologist joined us when we landed in India, and I became nominally responsible to him. I was thus subject to the rules of the Meyers-Machiz Visiting

Act. Passed when a group of American technicians was
caught in "black drag" in Addis Ababa, the law restricted
the travel of Americans serving abroad to places a hundred
miles from their post. It meant that I could go no farther
than Jodhpur.

I tried every means I knew to get to Bombay—I even
simulated a nervous breakdown. My superiors stuck to the
letter of the law. I could not quit my job and leave, since
I was penniless and pay was withheld until the end of our
mission.

And so a year after my escape from Jacksongrad, I
found myself still a prisoner, and as far from my goal
as ever.

Our work was difficult and apparently futile. We established a field infirmary in a little village called Pnho, a
cluster of crumbling huts through which ageless humans
and goats moved in dreamlike poverty. Many such villages
dotted the barren region, the poorest in Thar. Its inhabitants, the Gets, were one of the most primitive tribes of
the subcontinent. Cut off from the nation, even from their
fellow-Moslem neighbors, they lived their lives in desper-
ate apathy. The land was near-desert, beyond hope of
cultivation, sustaining only a few meager shrubs. There
were no natural resources except for the pits of natron
into which the Gets dropped their dead.

Disease was rife. A rapid survey, conducted immediately after our arrival, revealed the presence among the
scattered population of epidemic typhoid, endemic syphilis,
hyperendemic yaws, pseudo-endemic dog's disease, peri-
demic leishmaniasis, para-epidemic erysipelas, and even—
among certain eremites—exodemic dengue. We were
poorly equipped to meet such challenges. If modern drugs
cured many illnesses in their acute forms, they were less
effective against chronic cases, and they did nothing to re-

pair the unclean habits that fomented disease. To eradicate these habits our numbers were too small, and our time too short.

Besides indifference and filth, superstition complicated our task. It was impossible, for example, to perform even routine surgery because the natives would not tolerate anesthesia, which they believed to be a form of demonic possession. A person even locally anesthetized became a devil and was pitilessly expelled from the community. During our first week, a ten-year-old boy whose tonsils we had removed was driven into the waste land and, when he returned to his village, stoned to death. In cases of necessity, the Gets resorted to the services of vagrant popular surgeons, expert only in lithotomy and rhinoplasty, who performed their operations with extraordinary speed and, consequently, a minimum of pain. I saw one such operator, using the pretty leaf-shaped knives of his trade, remove a stone in little more than a minute. The studied technique of our doctors fell short of such feats.

Gilles Colon, the Frenchman whose assistant I was, devoted himself to the problem of anesthesia and after several months found a solution to it.

Among the stunted shrubs that grew in the region, there was one belonging to the elecampane family that the natives shunned as poisonous. Its leaves were decidedly narcotic. Dr. Colon discovered that the juice of its flowers was readily absorbed through the skin, producing a local numbness or, if applied copiously, a trancelike daze in which an illusion of consciousness accompanied a complete deadening of the nervous system. The only side effect was heavy sweating, notably from the extremities.

Dr. Colon saw in these attributes a hope of anesthetizing his Get patients. If elecampane essence were administered to a native who had been kept ignorant of its use, he might imperceptibly succumb to it.

The doctor decided to dispense his anesthetic as a spray, in an ordinary atomizer. The French word for this is *bombe*, and Dr. Colon called his relaxing atomizer a *bombe atonique;* but to the natives (most of whom, for historical reasons I never grasped, spoke French and not English), he pretended that the name was *bombe à tonique.*

Although testing of the *bombe* among us soon determined the quantities needed for local anesthesia, Dr. Colon wanted to try a maximum dose on one of us before using the extract clinically. I volunteered to be the guinea pig, but my hand had raised a fresh harvest of sores and Dr. Colon feared that so active an infection might influence the test. A psychiatrist named Nora Camping took my place. She was sprayed with enough plant essence to put her into a "conscious coma" for twenty-four hours.

The anesthetic was administered on the morning of May 15. By May 25, the medical post at Pnho was nonexistent, Dr. Colon was dead, and I, delivered from captivity, had left India.

A tribe called the Bhuris lives in the hills south of the Gets. While intelligent and industrious, they are as primitive as their neighbors in their beliefs: for instance, they hold that female feet are sacred because, pressed together, they create a replica of the *yoni*. Bhuri women uncover their feet only when they give birth, when they embrace their husbands, and when they die.

Dr. Colon anesthetized Nora Camping early in the morning. A little before noon, a Bhuri patient happened into her tent. During the day the psychiatrist was irregularly attended, and the native discovered her alone. She lay motionless on a cot, eyes staring upward, her naked extremities protruding from the sheet that covered her. The

Bhuri at first thought she was dead, but found her warm and breathing. Smitten at the sight of her pale feet with an ecstasy more holy than carnal, he knelt down by the bed to kiss and suck her toes. They tasted of an inhuman sweetness—the plant essence evidently flavored the sweat it provoked. The Bhuri half swooned, convinced that he had come upon a living goddess. Mastering his delight, he quietly left the tent and hurried home with news of the event.

That night he returned with eight strong youths. I was attending Nora, perhaps dozing, when they came: they surprised and soundlessly overpowered me. Bound and gagged, I was carried away with Nora to the Bhuris' village.

A few hours later disaster struck our camp.

In May the upper reaches of the Indus are swollen with Himalayan thaw. The bed of the river normally contains the seasonal increase—occasionally there is a minor flood.

A few days before my kidnaping, rains of unusual intensity began falling on the southern slopes of the Himalayas, doubling the volume of melted snow. The waters of the Indus rose precipitously. In the north, where the riverbanks are high, little damage was done, but the southern plain, basking in the end of the dry season, was subjected to the most terrible flood of its history. The mass of water moving south was so great that after overwhelming the valley of the Indus it backed into several of its tributaries, reversing their course and ravaging the territories they traversed.

Pnho, where we were stationed, lay on the Fara River. There it was only a gulley; downstream it became an intermittent tributary of the Indus; once, ages ago, it had been the true bed of the great river, which had shifted to the west in its epochal displacement.

The flooded Indus ran backward up the Fara, past the active stretch into the dry reaches where it had flowed thousands of years before. The natives of the arid country had no warning of their doom. On the night of May 15 the waters mounted the vacant riverbed like a tidal wave. They razed the village of Pnho in seconds, and our camp with it. Dr. Colon disappeared with most of our team; only the American survived to report the calamity.

Because the Bhuris live in hill villages, Nora and I were saved. We remained isolated with our captors for several days, amid prospects of catastrophe. Even Nora's divinity was eclipsed.

Gathered on their hilltops, the Bhuris counted few dead in the flood; but it endangered their very livelihood.

North of their hills was the Gets' waste land; to the south lay a moderately fertile plain where the Bhuris grazed livestock—their only wealth.

The floodwaters reached this plain as their momentum expired, immersing it without violence and turning it into a morass, in which thousands of cows and newborn calves were stranded. Unless they could recover the firm ground of the hills, they would soon die.

At first there was hope for them; during the night the waters were absorbed by the plain, only to rise the next day. A rhythm of ebb and flood, the delayed result of nightly rainfall on the upper Indus, set in for six days, frustrating the attempts of the cattle raisers to save their herds.

The Bhuris had descended in a body to meet the emergency. The men tried every method they could devise of carrying the helpless cattle to safety; invariably they ended up to their waists in mud. The women cut and hauled branches and reed fagots which they laid down as paths for the plaintive beasts, who found no footing. Children

slogged across the plain carrying fodder: there was little
of it in that season, and it soon gave out. The loss of
the entire herd seemed inevitable.

On the fifth day of the flood, the Kabul River, which was
also out of control, left its bed and broke a new channel
to the Indus south of Cherat. It swept a region with it,
bearing downstream whole parcels of land. I was told that
despite the universal desolation, thousands assembled along
the riverbanks to watch the water-borne parade—gardens, graveyards, hamlets, uprooted intact and floating
rapidly oceanward.

Now southwest of Cherat stood a famous hill called
Bhul Bholayan, the Maze (and by some, Bhulay-Huway
ki Bhul Bholayan, the Maze of the Forgotten). Bare,
stoneless, two hundred feet high and half a mile in circumference, the hill was inhabited by a colony of ants that
was supposed to be the largest in the world and thought
locally to be of divine origin.

In its deviation the Kabul River demolished Bhul Bholayan. Kept buoyant by their spongelike structure of ce-
mented passages, great fragments of the hill drifted south.
They reached the mouth of the Fara at the peak of the
daily flux and were carried up the river to the end of the
flooded region—that is, to the plain of stranded cattle.
When, at night, the waters subsided, fragments of Bhul
Bholayan were dispersed over the plain.

During the same night, for the first time in twenty-five
days, no rain fell on the upper Indus.

The following morning, on earth still soaked but no
longer submerged, a process of formication began. With
prompt industriousness, ants swarmed from the remains of
their hill to bore into the mud and build a new kingdom.
After only a few hours tan patches showed where their
labor had begun to aerate the ground.

For two nights more there was no rain, and the ants continued their excavation.

By the third day a crust of dried earth covered the plain. The natives led the calves over it to higher ground.

On the fourth day, six thousand cows were retrieved.

The rains then resumed, once more flooding the plain, and destroying the ant colony. Only two hundred cattle had perished.

Twelve days after the start of the flood, a group of tourists arrived in our village. Among them was an old friend, Carmen, the Marchesa di Nominatore. Greeting her, I discovered how exhausting the past weeks had been: she did not recognize me. When I told her my name, she embraced me tenderly:

"My poor darling! I shall take care of you now."

She had been lately in Bombay. I asked her for news of the "Sugars."

"I do know them, but they're gone—North Africa, I think."

Accepting her invitation, I left that evening. Nora stayed on to exploit her godhead.

Morocco

Although her name was Italian, Carmen was of German extraction. She descended from Ludwig Spanferkel, a fifteenth-century brewer ennobled by Albert the Wise, Duke of Bavaria-Munich. Spanferkel was the inventor of a brown beer that won the Duke's favor. The brewer had called it Nominator (declaring prophetically *"Cervisiam non nominabimus nos, sed nos seseque nominabit cervisia: Nominator nominetur"*), and Albert endowed him with the title *Herzog von Nominator*, raising him and his family to unexpected eminence.

Having made a fortune from their brewery, the Spanferkels invested it in new enterprises at home and abroad. One branch of the family settled in Florence, where they prospered in silk and Italianized their name. Later Nominatores extended the family interests to America, and Carmen's parents now divided their time between Tuscany and Trenton.

She had been a dear friend in my conservatory years. I told her what I had become; in the warmth of reviving affection she promised to help me complete my task.

In Bombay, we learned at the Ulek, Manis & Petis offices

that the directors had left for Tangiers. We soon followed them, flying to Morocco via Rome.

We landed late one evening. From the airport we took a
taxi to our hotel, a cluster of luxurious bungalows west of
the town, on the edge of an isolated beach. Tangiers revealed its presence by a bright glow cast up into the night,
and a faint but distressing roar.

Pointing toward the town, our taxi driver said as he left
us,

"*Aquí, bien. Allá, no poder pasar.*"

A few telephone calls were enough to locate the UMP
representatives. Early in the morning I drove into Tangiers.

Ordinarily the ride to their hotel would have taken
twenty minutes, but when we were about a mile from the
port my taxi was slowed by a tumultuous crowd that
thickened rapidly as we advanced. My driver turned
around before we were hemmed in, and tried another approach; we were blocked again. I was advised to proceed
on foot.

Doing so, I found the going no better—I had to pummel
and kick my way through a mass of reeling bodies. Although I passed close to the center of the crowd I did
not learn why it had gathered until I was clear of the
melee and back at my hotel.

Together with its fiscal privileges, Moroccan indepen-
dence ended the notoriety of Tangiers as a center of
pleasure. A year after being absorbed by the new state, all
but one of its "brilliant brothels," whose high-priced
chic was legendary, had closed down.

The exception was the Pension Macadam. Nationalized
by the royal government, it had remained a showplace of
elegant depravity. Spanish nobles, Russian tycoons and
fancy sports of every land still crossed the world to ride
in its famous elevator, in which the floors were indicated
not by numbers but by the names of glamorous tenants—

Lou, Jean, Jerry, Désiré(e), Babe. The populace of Tangiers treated these "Macadam Queans" as celebrities, and followed their careers with pride.

A week before my arrival, Babe, the greatest of the "Queans," relegated a performance of her "Dance of Endearment" to an understudy, Dominique. The latter made the most of her opportunity. She turned the act, a strip tease that should have lasted ten minutes, into a four-hour solo of such sustained power that the entire clientele of the Pension sat through it uncomplaining, neglecting their other appetites, and even their health—a Zurich banker was afterward found dead of myocardial infarct, his dulled eyes fixed on the cabaret floor.

The next day the girl again performed in the brothel. It was her last private appearance. News of her had spread through the city. Encouraged by agitators who declared that the masses had a right to their property, the people demanded to see her. Dominique quickly consented.

Ignorant of the event, I passed close to the Place Royale, where Dominique was dancing on a specially erected and festooned podium.

Her performance was then in its fifth uninterrupted day. Exalted by the glamour of adoration, which was cast up to her hour after hour in shouts and groans, Dominique had given herself over to her art. Until the last, she is said to have remained dazzlingly supple and strong.

When I passed, four of every five Tangerines had left their homes to see her. Several thousand men had assembled at the beginning, and as the days passed and knowledge of her heroic and crafty endurance grew, women and children swelled the crowd.

Fully dressed, Dominique had worn sixteen garments and ornaments. She shed four of them on the first day, three on each of the next four days, and at the end she

danced naked, shielded only by her hands and hair. Every
piece of her jewelry and clothing had been fastened with
an inextricable knot, from which one or several tassels
hung. The dancer's enchantment worked yeastily through
her audience while for hours she slowly tried, with shak-
ings and suave caresses, to pamper loose one cluster of
dangling strands. When the voluptuous ferment became
unbearable, the girl, turning away with a mild complicit
shrug, would draw from a scabbard fixed upright near
her a wicked blue scimitar, and slice the knot. The sword,
always visible to the crowd, gathered terrific significance
as the moment of its use approached; and each severing of
trivial cords fell on the tormented mass like a scourge, exciting hysterical shrieks, fits, faints, onsets of impotence,
confessions of unspeakable crimes, miraculous cures, num-
berless psychic and physical traumata, and the exchange
(settled by the unpredictable time of the event) of mil-
lions of francs among the slightly cooler-headed gambling
element.

(The cures were real. The sick and crippled quickly
emerged to try Dominique's influence, which worked
wonders among them. After her death—she collapsed at
sunset on the sixth day—she was proposed to Rome for
canonization.)

It took five hours for me to cross the impassioned
crowd, and I was lucky to come through unharmed. I
reached my destination, the Hotel de l'Univers et de Sfax,
in the early afternoon. At the desk I asked to see the
UMP directors.

"At noon they have leave for Italy—they can do nothing here with riot."

"I am a cousin of Dr. Roak," I said. "Do you have a
forwarding address?"

The receptionist wrote it out for me: *Fermo Posta, Atri
(Teramo), Italie.*

"I shall be joining Dr. Roak shortly. If anything was left behind . . ."

"The room is not cleaned. Accompany me, please, and we regard."

I climbed to the top floor and was shown into a room with a view of the harbor. I found only a sheet of paper with three words typed on it:

> *traîne*
> *pleure*
> *aigus*

The concierge suggested I take a motorboat back to my hotel, where I told Carmen of my misfortune. A day later we were on our way to Italy.

As we sat in our plane, which rose in a steep swerve over the African coast, my ears throbbed with discomfort in the changing pressure. I belched twice; my left ear started to ache. An hour later we endured a stormy interval, the aircraft wobbled mercilessly, and the pain gave way to an inaccessible itch and a clearly sounding high A. Finally, when the turbulence subsided, the A introduced an obsessive tune that unreeled itself inside my head until we landed:

Italy

In Rome I consented to have my ear examined. A doctor was called to our hotel, and he suggested that the infection in my hand might have spread. When he began examining my sores, I dismissed him.

After a night's rest, I set out for Atri. Carmen wanted to accompany me, but I went alone. An early morning train brought me to Pescara in time for lunch, after which I took a bus.

Toward the end of the drive, the winding road and an oppressive smell of oil and leatherette overcame me. Faint and retching, I was let off six miles from Atri, near Caduta Massi. I sank down on the embankment and vomited.

A peasant who had watched me incuriously, proved kind: he pointed out a shortcut into town.

The path took me across the famous battlefield, marked here and there with monuments to the dead, into the hills. It was a summery day. The country air sweetened the bitterness in my mouth, and feeling a little lightheaded, I walked on in growing ease.

A sudden excruciating pain in the lobe of my left ear

shattered my contentment. I shook my head, thinking I
had been stung; the pain increased. Hearing a voice behind
me, I turned to see a hawk-faced, black-haired man of
terrifying size emerging from a nearby grove. He carried
a slender fishing rod from which a slack line, dripping
slightly, rose to the side of my head.

"Whoa there!" he cried reassuringly. "Well, I knew the
black gnat was a great fly, but I didn't expect to catch anything *this* big."

Stopping near me, he continued: "Capeesh English?
You're American? I'm real sorry about that backcast, but
if it had to happen, it's just as well it was me that did it.
Don't you move and I'll repair the damage. First let me
introduce myself, Nathaniel Cavesenough of Bellevue
Hospital. Keep still now, and I'll make it as painless as I
can."

Taking from his lapel a large needle, which he charred
in the flame of a zippo, he began manipulating my ear
lobe.

"Say, that ear's infected." The hook came out with a
mild twinge. I had hidden my left hand abruptly; the doctor drew it forth and whistled.

"That's about the most disgusting mess I *ever* saw. What
do you mean walking around with a pestilential swamp on
the end of your arm?"

I turned away in a sweat. His disgust was fair. Fresh
sores and the seams of old ones gave my finger stumps a
carrion look.

"You've been *picking* at it." A frown replaced his smile.
"Now why did you do that? Turning a nuisance into a
catastrophe! Do you like misery? Do you enjoy being a
monster?"

"A 'nuisance'!" My voice broke. I told him of my disease.

"A *doctor* told you this is syphilis? If you've got syphilis, I'm Tutankhamen. It's yaws."

I laughed nastily and explained how I had contracted the disease, and that tests had confirmed the diagnosis.

"Uh huh. Now listen. Mothers don't catch syphilis from their children, not even congenital cases, right? Yaw germs and syphilis germs look the same under a microscope. Right? Chancres are a pain, but they don't itch. Right? Established yaws give positive Wassermanns. Q.E.D."

I did not answer.

"Since you insist on having a dread disease, I'll refrain from visible proof, which is: underneath all that you'll find a bed of little pink mushrooms—"

That was true. The doctors had never probed far enough into the foulness, but I had. I began to cry.

"O.K., O.K. Get it cleaned up and *forget* about it. This trip is turning into a busman's holiday. First Dr. Roak, then you. I'd prefer a few healthy trouts."

"Where?"

Dr. Cavesenough did not at first understand.

"Why, the doctor's in Atri—plans to visit the museum this afternoon and see the coins before they're removed. 'Hadrian's angels'—it turns out they're fakes."

When I started to thank Dr. Cavesenough he walked away, singing Dido's *Lament* in joyous falsetto. With a backward wave he disappeared among the trees.

I felt exhausted and should have rested awhile. But the present opportunity seemed sure, and at a quickened pace I strode on toward Atri.

It must have been four in the afternoon when I reached its outskirts. A pack of dusty black dogs loped out of town as I arrived. I traversed the steep maze of streets toward the Gothic superstructure of the cathedral—the museum, I knew, was next to it.

At the museum door a guard responded drowsily to my
inquiries. Yes, some foreign visitors had come in about ten
minutes ago. No, not just for the coins—the gardens and
cellars too. What cellars? I would see for myself.

"After big bock, door on right. Then door next to the
carrot. Straight ahead under crispy. Then you got no
choice."

My blank face must have discouraged him.

"Ah, ask Mrs. Acquaviva—she take them through."

I bought a ticket and hurried in.

Crossing a hall of gravestones and sarcophagi, I entered
a smaller room lit by a dirty skylight. Beneath it, enclosed
in glass and identified by a handwritten card as the *editio
princeps* of Rhazes the Physician, a folio incunabulum lay
open to the chapter *De Variolâ*. The book rested on a
white grocer's scale that registered twenty-two kilograms.

A double door stood open at the right end of the wall
facing the entrance. It led into a large high-windowed
gallery whose walls were crowded with paintings. At first,
searching among them, I could not find another door, then
saw that one was camouflaged by decoration—a painted
Egyptian scene. By it hung a copy of Caroto's *St. Roch
Showing His Inguinal Bubo*. The door yielded to my cau-
tious pressure.

The next room was windowless, lighted only by a dim
chandelier, which failed as I passed under it. The door
behind me shut with a snap. Turning back, I found it
locked.

I peered fearfully about the room. When my eyes had
grown used to the darkness, I distinguished a varied glow
on the far wall, high above the floor. Approaching it, I
recognized a familiar scene—the *Slumber Trio* from the
Palazzo Zen, painted in phosphorescent paints; but here
the musicians were naked, and their instruments had

changed into bodies or limbs, scrupulously obscene. The painting surpassed the Zen version, which it doubtless resembled by day. So witty a marriage of pornography and high art would have detained me, but remembering the guard's advice, "Straight ahead under crispy," I entered the darkness beneath the painting and groped my way through velvet curtains into the following room.

It was an enclosed terrace, walled on three sides with glass. Here "Hadrian's angels" were displayed—bright silver coins stamped with an image of the emperor touching his kneeling subjects (perhaps curing them of scrofula). Beyond, French windows opened onto a sunlit garden.

On a lawn fenced with cedars, a dozen children sat in a ring, whispering in turn to one another. I walked past them toward a gap in the row of trees. There, a path led off between slovenly hedges of yew. Unable to discover its direction over the hedge tops, I followed it in a large semicircle. At a point where another path joined it, I entered an arbor of cypresses. My heels pressed into grassless wet earth. There was a recumbent statue at the end of the arbor; its back was toward me, and of a worn inscription on its base I made out only the letters . . . *cirlcie* . . .

The alley ended there. I retraced my steps and took the other path at the arbor entrance. Symmetrically disposed, it reflected the semicircle of the first.

I heard voices ahead of me; then a door swung shut.

I broke into a run. The hedges ended on either side of an arched doorway that was set in the wall of a low stone building. Beyond the unlatched door a steep stairway slanted into darkness, with a glimmer of light at its foot.

Pressed against the wall, I descended. The air became steadily colder.

At the bottom I entered a huge cellar. Tiny windows

high in its vaults suffused the air with a bluish glow. Fat
white columns, with little space between them, rose on all
sides to the roof. There was a sour stench.

I was out of breath and giddy with weakness. Leaning
against one of the columns, I felt my arm sink into it. I
cried out and pulled myself free; my hand retained a palm-
ful of white ooze. Sniffing it, I learned that the columns
were made of cheese.

I had seen no one else in that sapphire milkiness, but my
shout had not gone unheard. Evelyn Roak appeared at the
far end of a row of cheeses, walking toward me. The
afternoon had been too much for my empty stomach and
harassed mind. Bitter fumes swirled into me, I fell senseless toward the blue flags of the cellar floor.

France

The fumes still pinched my nostrils when I woke up. Because my eyes were swathed in cloth I could see nothing; I heard quiet laughter.

I yelled, tugging at my blindfold. Steps approached, a woman said, *"Du calme, du calme,"* a hand pressed me against my pillows.

"What time is it?"

"I am your nurse. You are in a nice hotel in La Léchère."

"Who are you?"

"In the Alps—in Savoy."

I tried to jump up, but they held me. The woman spoke when I was still. "Here is Dr. D——. He will explain."

Another voice said, "Do not be upset.

"Professor Marr, whom I met last month, told me of your disease. I deduced the mistake made in the first diagnosis, and I reckoned that your yaws had lasted too long for ordinary treatment; but I know of a cure for them.

"You took four weeks to trace. I sent you a telegram in Rome—'Cure here urgent'—which arrived on the day of your excursion. Your friend telephoned the Atri police

about the time they retrieved you from the cheese cellars.
They gave my message to Dr. Roak and Dr. Cavesenough,
and my colleagues decided to send you to me at once. They
administered heavy sedation, and Signora di Nominatore
had a trained nurse bring you here. The Marchesa herself
could not come. Her mother is ill, and to be with her she
has flown to New Jersey.

"I am sorry you were not unbandaged when you awoke.
Mademoiselle, remove the dressing."

My eyes adjusted slowly to the light. The bedroom windows overlooked a narrow valley. Mountains on either
side rose steeply from the banks of a turbulent river, over
which hung a cloud of mill smoke, counterpart of the
bitter smell.

I got to my feet, took a step toward the window, tot-
tered and would have fallen; Dr. D——'s stout arms held
me up. I leaned on them with relief. The sight of his be-
whiskered face, cleft with a stained but compassionate
smile, convinced me that it was time to allow myself the
luxury of health.

Dr. D—— was himself ill; he suffered from chronic
hives. At least he called the eruptions hives, although they
were of a unique and mysterious sort. For twenty years
the condition had perplexed Dr. D—— and his colleagues;
meanwhile, he had found a remedy for its symptoms, if
not for their cause.

The pragmatical doctor had great faith in folk medicine,
and he had discovered in a hamlet near La Léchère a
healer or *rhabilleuse* able to relieve his inflammations. She
treated him with elecampane poultices of which she refused to disclose the recipe; nor had Dr. D—— been able
to analyze them.

Three centuries before, a West Indian slave with yaws

had come to Le Villaret, the hamlet where the healer lived. Others caught his disease, which had withstood the mountain climate to reappear in rare, often neglected cases that resembled mine. The *rhabilleuse* had cured one such case in 1919, and at Dr. D——'s request she agreed to treat me. He was sure the treatment would succeed. I professed skepticism, and was filled with hope.

I first needed another week's rest to recover my strength.

One day I recognized a new face among the hotel guests—Joan, the smuggler I had met in Venice. He had prospered during the past year and was retiring from the business. Wealth had not sullied his charm.

With six derelict invalids for company, I was happy to see him. I did not hide my feelings; he agreed to stay awhile.

The Cure

The *rhabilleuse* had told Dr. D—— that I must see human blood shed on the day of my cure. Early one morning we called at the hospital in Moutiers to attend a thyroidectomy.

In the operating room I was stationed at the foot of the table. Dr. D—— stood behind me. He explained the operation as it proceeded, naming in detail each tissue exposed. His care was wasted, for I saw in the surgical opening only a pocket of unarticulated gore.

We drove up to Le Villaret at sunset. It was the feast day of the local saint, and the population had assembled in the village square in celebration. We watched their festivities for an hour or so—the prettiest was a polka danced by couples skipping in circles back-to-back, their heads turned so that each dancer looked into his partner's face.

It was late at night when the *rhabilleuse* appeared. She was a tall woman, old but alert, with strong arthritic hands. We followed her into a yard or garden and at her behest waited in the darkness while she departed and returned in an invisible shuffle. Standing near us, she turned on a pocket flashlight, gave it to the doctor, and told him to direct its beam at her feet. On the small circle of illuminated earth she set a glass pitcher half-filled with water and dropped into it three handfuls of a yellow substance, desiccated petals of some flower. Dissolving, the yellow flakes produced a faint smell like that of violets; the water turned black.

At a sign from the woman, Dr. D—— turned off the flashlight. Her hands groped blindly over me until they found my hair, which she seized and pulled downward. I fell to my knees, my head pressed against my right shoulder. A hard tube was thrust into my left ear and warm liquid poured into it, overflowing on my face and neck. The *rhabilleuse* withdrew the tube; I heard it drop. She gripped my left arm, drawing it straight, and spilled the rest of the lotion over my outstretched hand. As it washed my sores the liquid stung slightly and glittered in the darkness, then fell in luminous gray puddles that slowly faded into the ground.

According to Dr. D——, I was soon stricken with "temporary confusional insanity." I remember a gloomy kitchen, with the doctor sitting next to me, patting my hand. The *rhabilleuse* was closing a small cork box that lay on her knees. It was lined with yellow silk and filled with sprigs of a single plant.

Dr. D—— drove me back to La Léchère at about one in the morning.

For a fortnight I washed my infections eight times a day with a clear solution that the old woman prescribed. By the thirteenth day my sores had dried up; at the end of three weeks they were scars.

Part Five

Love in the Mountains

My attachment to Joan grew stronger. He was delicate and reserved with me, but I did not think him indifferent.

A chance gesture undid his reticence.

We lay one afternoon among late spring flowers on a hill above the Isère. Joan was half asleep. Leaning over him, I grasped his wrists and gently squeezed them. Joan looked up, his eyes full of tears, and embraced me.

Only later could I explain the event.

Years before, Joan had served his smuggler's apprenticeship in the Pyrenees, carrying petty contraband between France and Spain. Once, with a consignment of twelve wrist watches, he met a woman in a town near the French frontier. She led him to a mountain field and there seduced him—he was still a boy, it was his first knowledge of love. Strapped to each forearm under his sleeves, the watches exerted throughout the encounter their leathery pressure.

When, seizing his arms, I recalled that tightness, the old astonishment revived. Caught by surprise, Joan's will yielded to mine.

One day Dr. D——, Joan and I had lunch together. We were very gay. Over coffee Dr. D—— declared pater-

nally, "You should get married." I said nothing. In a moment Joan leaned toward me and spoke with great earnest-
ness, "Mary, he's right. I cannot stand so much happiness."
(Joan called me by my middle name—Nephthys, he said,
was a mouthful of bones.)

I agreed. Dr. D—— found us a Defective Baptist minis-
ter. He was a stone-headed Hanoverian who had just arrived in the region, and he refused to leave his pursuit of
butterflies for even an hour. We went up to Courchevel
at his pleasure, and one day early in July were married at
dawn.

Convalescence

My thoughts soon slipped back into their usual rut, chiefly because of a conversation with Dr. D——.

"Do you know," he asked me, "why Dr. Roak was in Atri at the time of your accident?"

I shook my head.

"Three of the 'Sugars' had just decided to quit the UMP organization and start a business of their own.

"You know how rapidly the craze for pet nightingales has spread since last year. My colleague (who was once also my patient) found that the birds can be easily taken with snares baited with the furry tips of cattails. But not ordinary cattails: only those half-rotted by the tiny worms that are found in Atrian cheese."

I asked Dr. D—— why Evelyn Roak had come to him for treatment.

"Not treatment, diagnosis. It is a perilous condition, brought on by bad teeth. The body's normal production of antibodies has been permanently upset. If every infection is treated rapidly, there is not too much danger. For Dr. Roak the risk is exposure to a serious disease when already subject to an infection, even one as mild as a carbuncle: the infection would exhaust the antibody reaction, leaving nothing for the disease, and the rest would be up to the undertaker."

It was on the same occasion that Dr. D—— persuaded me to turn my dental experience to account.

The day came when, my convalescence over, Joan and I left La Léchère. Calling to say good-bye, I asked Dr. D—— for his bill.

"Twelve thousand dollars, please."

Grateful as I was, I protested. Dr. D—— answered,

> *"Empta solet care*
> *multum medicina juvare;*
> *Si quae detur gratis,*
> *nil affert utilitatis."*

"But that isn't true. I'm already cured."

"Not true? My dear, in medicine the truth is a goal one cannot attain."

The Journey to Sfax

I had decided to settle in Nivolas-Vermelle. It is a "Gothic factory" town not far from Lyons, where I was to resume my dental instruction, and lacked a resident dentist. The marshes surrounding the town hold the richest growth of cattails in Europe or Africa; and while I did not seriously count on such a circumstance in my pursuit of "Doctor Roak," who had disappeared from sight, it made my choice easier.

By the end of summer we had moved into a comfortable house overlooking the town. At the beginning of September, I enrolled in the newly founded Institut King Dri de Chirurgie Dentaire: to my satisfaction, the school promptly awarded me a dental technician's license. My mornings were spent at school and the rest of my time in Nivolas-Vermelle. I equipped and opened an office in two rooms of our house. In honor of the *rhabilleuse* I decorated it with cork and yellow silk.

One day toward the end of October my maid announced, "*Y a une dame rauque désire vous voir.*" I told her to admit the visitor, and in a moment Evelyn Roak strode into the office. She looked as handsome and young as ever. On her left wrist she wore a charm bracelet from which hung, among images and coins, two small but human bones.

I thought, "I'm the queen of the castle!"

"Hello, Miss Wassermann," she said, kissing me on both cheeks.

"Hello, Miss Krafft-Ebing."

"Still black as a Newgate knocker! None of that, ducks: I've come to make up. Where's your old man?"

"He flew to North Africa yesterday on business."

"*Aethera novum homo transvolans*—too bad. I wanted to meet him. He's not going to Sfax?"

"No—isn't there a smallpox epidemic?"

"I'll say—nine hundred cases in a week. *I* was there collecting bird food." She touched wood. "Freshly mutated and ambitious virus, leading to, as one straight-faced medico informed me, 'zingular pleural gombligations,' accompanied by strangury and dissolution of the soul. And speaking of epidemics, in Paris I heard of a sweet one from—guess who?"

"Who."

"Bea Fod."

"*That* sexpot?"

"Neppy!"

"The last I heard of her she'd been put away for public indecency—she was caught in Rye, on a street where there'd been a boys' day school. The school had closed, but Bea still hung around to bewilder an occasional fugitive—sad, romantic Bea!"

"They released her. She now tours the world in pursuit of medical atrocities."

"Wait till she reaches India!"

"Wasn't it heaven? 'A hundred and one blunt instruments, of which the chiefest is the hand.'"

"Sesame!"

"Enemas of ethereal oils!"

"Our patients insisted on calling us by the names of the medicines we 'invented'—meet Bella Donner."

"Let me tell you about Bea's epidemic. Last year she was 'doing' the Appalachians and found this town on the Essuimantic full of diseased rats. The disease made them very brave—they attacked the inhabitants in broad daylight, jumping on them and biting chunks out of their flesh. The bites never healed, and never grew worse; they also turned white. Not skin-colored: white."

"And Bea herself?"

"For one thing she's had her face remade (her brother keeps saying

'The youthful hue
Sits on thy skin like morning glue,'

to everyone's embarrassment). For another, she's compiling a monumental work out of her medical expedition, a work 'for the ages.' It's supposed to justify her and put her persecutors to shame. She says the best vengeance is immortality. And do you remember Marion Gullstrand? *She's* cleared herself—evidently that untimely ripping was an improved kind of Smellie delivery."

"Do the babies concur in this version?"

"Cuz, I'm glad you're happy. You're a big girl at last—you were such a whiner! Change isn't usually so beneficial. Can you believe it, I think daily of our music. Why couldn't *I* have had talent? But perfecting the past is a medieval jag, isn't it . . . perhaps some day we'll be friends —impersonal friends?"

I did not answer. Evelyn looked about her.

"A spick place. Do you still have the phosphorescent family bed lamps? I hadn't heard you were a dentist." She laughed, a little contemptuously.

"Only half one for the time being. But perhaps I might look at *your* teeth?"

"If you like. Please to notice my lower left molars and the small canyon made by your candy-bomb—idiot!" She said this smiling as she approached the surgical chair. Sitting down, she kissed me on the mouth and gave me a slap rather hard for play.

I stepped away to turn on the overhanging lamp and attach my eye-mirror, grateful for such screens. Evelyn lay back, openmouthed and indifferent.

Waiting for my pulse to slacken, I probed her mouth. On the left side of the jaw a slight swelling caught my attention. When I touched it Evelyn started.

"Uh ah?"

"Food caught next to the gum," I explained. With a pair of tweezers I pretended to remove the imaginary fragment.

I was ready to satisfy my patience—gas, straps and drills were at hand. Now a new possibility arose. I was sure that an abscess had formed under the gold of Evelyn's damaged teeth. I put my hand on her forehead: the skin was dry and hot.

"How have you felt lately?"

"Well, cuz. Except my back's an ague from so much travel, my nose itches incessantly, I've had terrible nightmares, and when I wake up, four beasts wait at the corners of my bed. They are not my type."

"When were you in Sfax?"

"Most of this month."

She had not left untouched. The symptoms were classic.

"The gum is irritated. I'll give you a shot of antibiotic to stop any infection."

Doing so, I used a solution of half the required strength.

It would temper the pain and swelling for a day or two, nothing more.

Evelyn looked anxious when she rose from the chair. I reassured her and gave her, "for any residual discomfort," two of Laurence's anesthetic thorns, which I had saved through all my wanderings.

Then I relinquished my opponent to her stars.

There is a print of Sfax, a belated *image d'Epinal*, over my office door.

The picture shows, within a border of linked cucumbers, a bird's-eye view of the town and its environs. The coloring of the print is pale or garish, its drawing generally crude, with a few elegant details. I do not remember where I bought it—perhaps it was already in the house when we moved in.

The print entertainingly depicts native and colonial life.

In its lower right-hand corner stands the Arab town, the citadel or casbah. Its ramparts form a neat rhombus whose upper and lower edges are horizontal, while the sides lean slightly to the left—the outside of the two near walls and the inside of the two far ones are thus visible. Crenelated towers rise at the four corners. The fortifications are colored ochre.

The casbah has three gates, identical arches of green and white tile, one in each wall except the nearest, which is bare. A crowd of Arabs is passing through the gate in the left-hand wall. The other entrances are vacant. Far to the right, at the very edge of the picture, a caravan approaches the town. It will penetrate the lateral arch into a large street lined with shops, between which piles of vases, pots and wicker-covered flasks complete an irregular façade.

The houses in the casbah have flat roofs enclosed by

low walls. Many of these walls are draped with rugs, mottled patches of dark red and blue. The houses are beige-colored, with black doors and windows. Like the adjacent streets, their roofs and yards are empty, except for one large courtyard where some private festivities are taking place. There, three girls dance in front of a group of seated men; veiled women watch from doorways; an earthen oven shaped like an igloo emits blue feathers of smoke. The robes of the Arabs, here as elsewhere, are white, their complexions gray.

Beyond the casbah, the native port appears. Green fishing boats are drawn up at its quay, their bows pointing inland, their yellow sailless masts reclining at a queer angle. Nets hang along the shore between conical piles of pink sponges. Among them a few Arabs sit looking out to sea.

The foreign port lies immediately to the left. At its center a long pier reaches into the water: it is studded with bollards; hawsers and chains, bales and kegs are stacked along it; launches and a coastal freighter are moored at its sides. Several hundred people are crowded onto the tip of the pier. They are mostly Europeans. The men are dressed in white, the women in long gowns of mauve and pale yellow.

The colonial town recedes from the port in regular blocks of spaced white buildings. On a line with the pier, following the vertical axis of the picture, runs the main avenue. It is bordered with double ranks of young palm trees, behind which numerous Europeans have gathered in meticulous files. From the windows above them watching heads emerge. Bright tricolors hang at intervals along the street, and red white and blue bunting has been strung in cordons along the dark green trees.

Farther inland, near the left-hand edge of the print,

beyond a water cistern marking the limit of the town, there is an army camp, a square of pale blue tents. Three sentinels in khaki stand watch on its outskirts.

Between the camp, the new town and the casbah lies a space of clear ground. On it two parades are taking place. To the left, a column of French soldiers marches toward the crowded avenue of the European quarter— white-capped spahis on red and brown horses, a Zouave band in blue jackets and scarlet chechias, and Zouave foot soldiers. To the right, under the casbah wall, surrounded by hundreds of watching Arabs, a line of Berber horsemen executes a *fantasia*. Caught in mid-career, the black horses stiffly gallop, the riders twist excitedly, brandishing upright rifles that discharge minute red and black V's.

Along the bottom of the print, a tranquil strip of countryside contrasts with the animation of the parades. The land is flat. Gardens open among spreading orchards of olive, almond and lemon; tracts of vine adjoin the villas. There are few human figures. A shepherd sits against an olive tree, his flock grazing about him. Not far from their stepladder, left standing in the branches of an almond tree, nut harvesters sleep in an orchard. The shadowed alleys of the necropolis are empty.

Country, harbor and town fill the lower third of the picture; beyond is sea and sky.

Parallel to the shore, in indigo water, five gray ships ride at anchor. Only their hulls are plain, for from them, outshining the rest, an effusion of brilliant fire issues—above a couch of pinwheels and squibs, while huge tourbillions at either side shoot into violet spirals, three salvos of rockets between stamp fans of silver on the darkness, yielding as they rise galactic profusions, their garnitures of bombs, balls, snakes and fiery snow. The labyrinth of their colors sets a dense clarity against the blankness of the night.